Little Demon *finds investigator Plant back in the iconic paradise of Byron Bay, hired by ageing rock 'n' roll journalist Rock Richmond whose computer with his history of the alternative communes has been stolen. Plant's rural retreat is invaded by conspiracy theorist Fullalove, who figures Richmond had been writing about rumoured Cold War arms caches and secret militias. Plant's inquiries involve Rock's wife, a barrister specializing in drug cases, his girlfriend the mysterious Madimi, and caravan park owner and rifle club president Jake, a former army officer who used to run a commune.*

LITTLE
DEMON

Also by Michael Wilding

Fiction

Aspects of the Dying Process

Living Together

The Short Story Embassy

The West Midland Underground

Scenic Drive

The Phallic Forest

Pacific Highway

Reading the Signs

The Man of Slow Feeling – Selected Short Stories

Under Saturn

Great Climate

Her Most Bizarre Sexual Experience

This is for You

Book of the Reading

Somewhere New: New and Selected Stories

Wildest Dreams

Academia Nuts

Wild Amazement

Superfluous Men

The Plant novels:

National Treasure

The Prisoner of Mount Warning

The Magic of It

Asian Dawn

In the Valley of the Weed

Documentary

The Paraguayan Experiment

Raising Spirits, Making Gold & Swapping Wives: The True Adventures of Dr John Dee & Sir Edward Kelly

Wild Bleak Bohemia: Marcus Clarke, Adam Lindsay Gordon and Henry Kendall: A Documentary

Memoir

Wild & Woolley: a Publishing Memoir

Growing Wild

Non-fiction

Milton's Paradise Lost

Cultural Policy in Great Britain (with Michael Green and Richard Hoggart)

Marcus Clarke

Political Fictions

Dragons Teeth: Literature in the English Revolution

Social Visions

The Radical Tradition: Lawson, Furphy, Stead (The Colin Roderick Lectures)

Studies in Classic Australian Fiction

LITTLE DEMON

MICHAEL WILDING

ARCADIA

This is a work of fiction. Names, characters, places and incidents are the products of the author's imagination or are used fictitiously. Any resemblance to actual events, locales, or persons, living or dead, is entirely coincidental.

To Carl Harrison-Ford

Chapter 1

Rock Richmond stood at his picture window gazing at the view. His view. He looked across the coastal plain below to the ocean. It was a seriously expensive view. Even in hard times. Plant tried putting a price to it but gave up: as soon as you had settled on a figure, the figure would prove inadequate. Every moment it was going to be worth more, or less. He settled for a generic description: a multi-millionaire's view, to allow for capital appreciation or depreciation, nanosecond by nanosecond. Not that he imagined Rock Richmond was a multi-millionaire. As far as he knew. He was clearly not short of serious wealth. But journalists were hardly in the multi-millionaire category. Or were they? Richmond's casual gear signalled expensive taste, and the very latest in up-to-the-minute fashion and accessories. Year by year it would change. And Rock Richmond, chronicler of style, would change with it.

'I've been robbed,' Rock Richmond said.

'I'm sorry to hear that,' Plant said.

Even the seriously rich had their little problems sent to try them.

'You can spare me the condolences,' Rock said. Genially enough. He was nothing if not genial. 'Like trying to report your credit card's been stolen and getting some call centre in Bombay. "Oh, sir, sorry sir, most terribly sorry to hear it, sir, how very unfortunate, sir."'

It was not a bad Indian accent. He had talent as a mimic. He followed it with a master of the universe impression.

'I don't want condolences, I want action.'

'What sort of action did you have in mind?' Plant asked.

'You're the investigator, you tell me.'

'I imagine the police are on the case.'

'And a fat lot of help they are.'

Plant looked at the view. Cape Byron jutted out into the ocean. The lighthouse glistened white, iconic seal of desirable lifestyle and material achievement.

'You have no clues as to who might be responsible?'

'Clues!' Rock Richmond said. 'What do you think this is? The Friday night murder mystery? Someone broke in and took the computer.'

'That's all that was taken?'

'And the flash drive back-up, yes. It's quite enough.'

'No jewellery?'

'I don't wear any.'

'Your wife's? Are you married?'

'No and yes.'

'No and yes?'

'No, her jewellery wasn't taken; yes, I am married.'

'No electronic gear, television, record player, camera?'

'No.'

'Well, that's a clue,' Plant said. 'It would seem to rule out the usual junkie robbery.'

'I already told you, all they took was the computer.'

'So that suggests it was someone who knew what he wanted. Or she.'

'Yes. A computer.'

'Or the contents.'

Rock Richmond beamed a smile of self-satisfaction. Self-importance, even. He was a writer. Journalist. Television talking head. Award winner. Some years back, but still, he had been a significant figure. And still was. A writer. Some things could not be taken away. His books were ranked in rows in the bookshelf opposite the view.

'They didn't steal your books,' Plant said.

'No,' Rock Richmond said.

There was a momentary chill in the geniality as Rock Richmond gave him an icy look. To have your works stolen was bad: but not to have them stolen, to have them rejected and left behind was something else again.

'They didn't steal the paintings, either. Not your cultured sort of thief.'

Ranked along the wall above the bookcase were a Hazel Dooney, a Martin Sharp, a Kate Briscoe, a Peter Powditch, a Carmen Ky, a Garry Shead, a Chris Barry. Gender balanced, slightly favouring the feminine. Made in Australia.

'What about back-up?'

'I told you, they took the flash drive.'

'Where was it kept?'

'Beside the computer.'

Plant nodded. No point saying that was not the best place to have kept it. And there was a certain genial self-satisfaction about Rock Richmond's admission, as if he had a second back-up stored somewhere else.

'But I have a second back-up stored somewhere else,' he said.

'And they didn't get that.'

Rock Richmond grinned a toothy, full-lipped whiskery grin. 'No, they didn't.'

'So,' Plant said, 'apart from the loss of the computer, which presumably insurance will cover, what's the problem?'

'What's the problem?' Rock Richmond said, his voice up an octave or so.

'Well, if nothing is irretrievably lost ...'

'That's not the point.'

'Maybe you'd better tell me what is the point,' Plant said.

Rock Richmond nodded.

'So what were you were working on?'

'You know who I am, I imagine,' Rock Richmond said.

'Journalist,' Plant said.

'Writer.'

'You've moved up in the world,' Plant said.

Rock Richmond swung his gaze back from the view and fixed a pair of beady eyes on Plant. Then he gave his relaxed smile and fruity chuckle.

'I don't do a lot for the papers these days,' he said.

'I can't say the papers do a lot for me these days, either,' Plant said.

'No, well ...'

'So you were working on a book.'

Rock Richmond gave his expansive smile.

'I was. I am.'

'Can you tell me what it's about?'

A tricky question with contemporary creative types, risking the response that it was not *about* anything, it simply was. Is.

But Rock Richmond smiled and swept his arm round, the expansive gesture to go with the smile.

'This,' he said.

'This?'

'The alternative.'

'The alternative,' Plant said in measured tones. He

looked around the room, the stylish furnishings, the pricey paintings on the wall, the expensive leisure gear with which Rock Richmond was draped.

'The counter-culture.'

'Go on,' Plant said.

'This is where it began. Right here.'

'Here?'

'Well, not precisely *here*,' Rock Richmond said. 'Not this precise house. Which wasn't built then. But this region. This is where the alternative culture began. And developed. And flourished. Byron. Mullum. Nimbin.'

'And you're writing about it?'

'I was here. I lived through it. I observed it. It was my life.'

'And you're writing an autobiography.'

'Not as such. Not exactly as such. A spiritual autobiography in a way, I suppose.'

'So what is it exactly you're writing?'

'A history of the counter-culture. In all its manifold aspects. The communes. Environmental awareness. The New Age. Sustainability. The politics. The music.'

'The writing?'

'The writing. Of course.'

'I see.'

'It's big, I agree.'

'Yes.'

'It's never been done.'

'Really?'

'Not properly. Not inclusively.'

'And this is what was stolen?'

'Well, everything was stolen. Everything on the computer. But this is what I'm working on currently. This is the big project.'

'And someone knew about it and stole it.'

'So it seems.'

'Could anyone have known about it? Have you spoken to anyone about it?'

'I've been interviewing people.'

'For the book?'

'Yes, for the book.'

'And you told them it was for a book?'

Rock Richmond smiled. 'Of course.'

'How many?'

'How many what?'

'How many people have you interviewed?'

'Oh, lord,' he said.

'How long have you been working on it?'

'In one sense all my life. All my adult life, anyway.'

'And in another sense?'

'A year or so, eighteen months maybe.'

'So you've interviewed a lot of people?'

'Quite a few. I'm pretty thorough when I do a job.'

'But you've got your own memories, too. It's not just interviews.'

'Absolutely,' Rock Richmond said. 'I was here.'

'Living it.'

'In part,' Rock Richmond agreed. 'In large part, yes.'

'But in fact nothing has been stolen.'

'Everything was stolen,' Rock Richmond said.

'I'll put it in a different way,' Plant said. 'Nothing has been lost.'

'They took the lot.'

'But you've got back-ups of everything.'

'Fortunately.'

'So nothing's lost.'

'Well, everything and nothing.'

'So what exactly do you need me to do?'

'Find it.'

'I see,' Plant said. 'But you don't need it back to carry on with your book. You've still got the materials.'

'That isn't the point,' Rock Richmond said.

'So what is the point?' Plant asked. Politely. As politely as you could ask that sort of question.

'I don't want them popping up somewhere.'

'The materials?'

'Exactly.'

'When you say popping up ...' Plant said.

'I don't want them turning up in print. Under somebody else's name. Or my own name, for that matter. This project is strictly under wraps.'

Was this mad megalomania, Rock Richmond's delusions of grandeur, imagining his material was so good that someone would want to sell it on? It had never seemed that good to Plant. Or to anyone Plant knew. Indeed, there didn't seem to have been that much of it around, lately.

'It's a hot property. I can't afford to have choice gobbets served up before I'm ready. The publicity has to be properly coordinated to get the most out of it.'

'The most of what? Publicity? Or money?'

'I don't have anything against money, do you?' Rock Richmond asked. Chronicler of the alternative.

'Not at all.'

'So. This book if properly marketed could be worth megabucks.'

'Megabucks,' Plant said.

'Zillions. I want to tie up newspaper serialisation. I

don't want chapters popping up and spoiling that deal. I want to sign up a television doco. I don't want someone going in there with my material and grabbing it. And I don't want someone going through the text and taking out the scoops.'

'Scoops,' Plant said. 'That's a word I haven't heard for a long time.'

Rock Richmond gave him a look of weary contempt, behind which the fear of archaism fluttered anxiously.

'There are things in my manuscript that no one has ever dreamed of.'

'Really.'

'You'd better believe it. Revelations. World-shattering stuff.'

'World-shattering.'

'You heard it here,' Rock Richmond said.

'So it's not just a piece of local history.'

'It certainly is not.'

'So what are the world-shattering revelations?'

'Classified,' Rock said. 'They're under wraps till publication. I don't want any word getting out.'

'And you think with the burglary it might.'

'It better not.'

Plant looked suitably serious.

'That's why I'm hiring you.'

'I see.'

'You've got media connections. Research assistance. Investigative reporting.'

Plant nodded modestly. That was what his card proclaimed.

'Use them,' Rock Richmond ordered. 'Put the word round that there's material been stolen. Alert the features editors and commissioning editors so they don't sign it up from someone else. Tell them I'll sue if they do.'

'And let you know who the someone else is?'

Rock Richmond grinned. 'That would be interesting,' he said.

'And important?'

He shook his head.

'I'm not into retribution,' he said. 'I'm not planning to cut off anyone's hand. I just don't want the material coming out unauthorised. I don't want it coming out under someone else's name. I don't want the exclusives leaking before I've teed them up. Your job is to stop any of that happening.'

'And as for tracking down the villains?'

'Why not? You can nose around. See what you can sniff out.'

'The one might lead to the other,' Plant said.

'The one what?'

'If the material is offered somewhere, that might point to who's doing the offering.'

'Natch,' Rock Richmond said, giving his approving smile.

'I can do it,' Plant said. 'No problem.'

'That's my boy.'

'What about issuing a press release? That way you'd hit all the media and they'd be alerted to look out for the material.'

In fact he didn't really need Plant, he could do that himself. 'Am I talking myself out of a job?' Plant asked himself. But no, he wasn't.

'I don't want to do that.'

'It would be publicity. Writer burglarised. Always good

for a story. Get you in the public eye.'

'Exactly what I don't want. Not till the book's in the shops.'

'It might whet people's appetite.'

'No.'

'No?'

'No. Boredom factor. Counter-effective if you do the publicity too soon.'

'Fair enough,' Plant agreed.

'And apart from anything else it gives the wrong signals. People start to think you're a victim or incompetent. They start to think you've lost it. Having delusions or something.'

'Fair enough.'

'And it muddies the waters. I just want to get on with the job. I don't want a lot of publicity about it while I'm doing it. I want to be able to interview people quietly. Discreetly. If there's a whole lot of media chatter they're likely to clam up. These sort of people up here. They'll see it as media exploitation or something. That's why they became the alternative in the first place. No, it's much better my name's kept out of it and you just put the word around the press and television to watch out for the stolen materials.'

Chapter 2

'How did they get in?' Plant asked.

'Forced the door. Splintered the frame.'

'What about the burglar alarm?'

'What burglar alarm? We're not in the inner city here.'

'Looks like you are, now,' Plant said.

'I don't think so,' Rock Richmond said. 'It was just a one-off.'

'When did it happen? Day or night?'

'Day.'

'And you were out.'

'Yes.'

'Do you think someone knew your movements? Or were they watching the place?'

'It would be hard to watch the place without being noticed. You don't see too many cars parked along the road here.'

'So where were you? You and your wife.'

'Wife at work. Me, oh, I don't know, out somewhere or other.'

'So we can assume they were professional.'

'Just lucky,' Rock Richmond said.

'You think?'

'I can't see why professionals ...' He laughed his throaty, engaging laugh. 'I don't think they were professional writers stealing material, if that's what you're getting at. It hardly works like that. But once they'd got it someone might have seen a use for it, sell it on, you know.'

Plant didn't really. It didn't sound at all likely.

'Do you think they knew what you were working on and wanted that specifically? Or they just wanted to find out what you were working on? Or they were looking to take whatever it was you were working on? Or they just wanted a computer?'

Rock Richmond brooded.

'You're the investigator. No idea myself. If they took the computer, you'd think they would have taken the rest of the electronic gear.'

'Usually they take all that anyway,' Plant said, 'to make it look like a real job.'

'What do you mean, a real job? You saying this wasn't real, I dreamt it or something?'

'I'm sure you didn't dream it,' Plant said.

'So what are you getting at?'

'Well, if they were just after what you were writing, who are they likely to be?'

'You tell me.'

'Usually incidents like that are security or special branch. Is there any security angle on this? Are you on file somewhere?'

'Journalists are always on file,' Rock Richmond said, somewhat smugly, Plant felt.

'Except for the ones collaborating with the agencies.'

'Probably them, too,' Rock Richmond said. 'Nothing like keeping tabs on your own chaps.'

'And you?'

'Me?'

'Do you have a history of collaboration? Or a history of subversion?'

Rock Richmond smiled. 'If I had, I wouldn't be telling

you, would I?' he said. 'Either way,' he added.

'So could there be a security angle?'

Rock Richmond shrugged.

'So who else would want to steal your immortal words?'

'Someone from the old alternative, maybe.'

'Someone wanting to write their own history?'

'Why not?'

'Or someone with something to hide, wanting something not to come out.'

'That's a possibility.'

'Are there things like that in the book?'

'Hard to tell. Hard to know what people go funny about and don't want mentioned. Could be something trivial. Some domestic incident. Who was sleeping in whose sleeping bag.'

'Is there a lot of that?'

'It was a time of free love,' Rock Richmond said.

'Ah,' Plant said.

Rock Richmond smiled with sanctimonious self-satisfaction. Plant smiled along with him. The best of times swirled up and coalesced and dissolved around them.

'Perhaps that explains it all.'

'Perhaps it does,' Plant agreed.

Plant stood at the columned doorway, being graciously farewelled, when a current-model black BMW all-wheel-drive SUV drew up in a satisfying crunch and spray of gravel alongside the somewhat classic silver Porsche Carrera already parked there, and Plant's close to bottom-of-the-line Hyundai.

'My wife,' Rock Richmond said, with a touch of pride and a touch of fear.

She emerged as elegantly as you can emerge from an all-wheel-drive, dropping to the ground in free fall, serious black suit and heavy-duty black leather briefcase, skirt riding up over sheer black-stockinged thighs.

'Darling,' Rock Richmond called across.

She raised her left hand momentarily, snapped the fingers down in a notional wave, and came towards them, or towards the door they happened to be standing in front of.

'This is Plant,' Rock Richmond said, 'he's helping with the robbery.'

'Good,' she said, and walked past them into the house.

'Is she a journalist too?' Plant asked.

'Absolutely not,' Rock Richmond said. 'Legal eagle.'

'Solicitor?'

'High flying barrister, don't you know.'

Maybe that explained the house. The view. The air of wealth. It was a good sign. Not that Plant had ever disputed that all property was theft. Nor did he think that being wealthy meant that you were a nicer person. It just meant that he might get paid without too much trouble. Unless Mr and Mrs Richmond ran separate bank accounts. And he wouldn't be surprised at that.

Rock Richmond had been big once. Quite big, anyway. Forty-something years ago. He had been a regular face on television for a while, interviewing visiting celebrities. He had written about rock concerts and jazz festivals, surf carnivals and bicycle races, the renaissance of the movie industry and the death of the movie industry and more in the old broadsheets. Not that anybody much interested in rock or surfing had ever read the broadsheets. He had syndicated pieces on environmental activists and New Age gurus, natural health remedies and circuses, in women's magazines and lifestyle monthlies. He had reviewed film and television and books in the old weeklies. For a few years. After a while he had produced the odd book.

Plant called in at the local library and checked Rock out on-line. There were entries on him on a number of sites. And there were more books listed than Plant remembered. Indeed, they were not remembered, he had never heard of them. But there they were, the gaps between them longer each time, the last one a few years ago. The biographies of a couple of television soap stars. The corporate history of a couple of corporations. A novel. Ah well, Plant reflected, you couldn't hold writing a novel against someone.

Whatever was keeping Rock Richmond in comfort was not royalties from his books. Family money, perhaps. Or the barrister wife. It was hard to believe that anyone had stolen Rock Richmond's work in progress with a view to its market value. It was hard to believe anyone would want to steal it for any reason. But such mysteries, Plant told himself, are your bread and butter. Not that he ate bread and butter much any more. Bread gave him indigestion and people said butter was bad for you, but there again now they were starting to say it wasn't in fact as bad as they'd been saying it was.

He drove down to the beach and sat on the sand and watched the dolphins playing. It looked like they were playing. Though they could have been gobbling up little fishes. But there they were, just beyond the breaking surf, not even bothering to catch a wave. Not that it was much of a surf. They wallowed around, breaking the surface of the water. Plant watched them and relaxed. Eventually he would go back and start phoning up the media on Rock Richmond's behalf, while carefully not mentioning Rock Richmond's name. He wondered at that. Was it diffidence? Was Rock that rare writer who didn't like to put his name around? Plant rather doubted it. Was it less diffidence than fear? But fear of what? Was it maybe the case that he hadn't actually written that much yet? If anything at all. Notes, maybe. Lots of contact numbers. Jottings. But maybe when he said he was writing a book he was like many writers and would-be writers, he was getting ready to write a book, and putting off the awful moment. Was he afraid he might never get round to it? Or never complete it?

It was possible. But Rock Richmond had not struck Plant as someone prone to self-doubts. If he said he was going to write a book he would probably do it. With no fears or anxieties. Which suggested the fear, if it was fear, came from something else. He had mentioned revelations. It was hard to imagine what they could be. What could be of interest forty-something years later? But maybe he had come across something. Maybe that was why the computer and the back-up files had been stolen. Someone wanted to know what he had been writing, what he had discovered. Just wanted to know, or wanted to stop its publication? Yes, there were a number of questions he could follow up with Rock Richmond. Once he had done the media alert. Funny how people who hired you never quite told you everything you needed to know. There was always something else, some important little piece of information they had managed to mislay. You always had to go back and ask a few more things. Ah well, Plant reflected, that was the nature of the work.

Chapter 3

Plant headed inland towards Nimbin. The two stoned birds principle. He needed some dope and he could check out Rock Richmond with Max. Max had lived there since near the beginning of time. Alternative time. Before that it had been dairy farmers and before that the Great Dreaming. The trees fluttered their leaves with anticipation, stands of bracken quivered, the morning sun tinged the wisps of grass golden. Dope was in the air, its energy pulsing across the hills. The resin hung drowsily over the fields, down in the valleys the morning mist exuded a cannabis-saturated dew. It was an amazing drive. Plant felt his spirits lift.

Max was always reliable. Not precisely a connoisseur, which would have made it all too affected and twee. Nor a mad experimenter, which would have encouraged hydroponics and adulteration with additives and manipulation with genetic engineering. But someone with a sense of traditional values, someone who valued a quality product, like an old vigneron of a vanished age. Whether he grew it himself or bought it in Plant never knew. Some things were best not known, certainly not inquired about. All that mattered was that he held a quality product. And traded quality gossip. You wanted information, you had to buy a deal of dope. You wanted dope, you had to trade your bit of information.

There was an etiquette about buying dope. You couldn't just walk in, slap your money down, and leave. There had to be a little tea, a little chat, a shared joint, maybe, and talk about this and that. Max's this and that was always informative. He had the local historian's love of telling detail. He remembered sites and dates with an antiquarian exactitude. He knew the threading interconnections of relationships and ownerships, and would take you through them meticulously as you shared the joint, admired its quality, and intimated that if he had a deal of that available you would take it.

They sat at the kitchen table, old scrubbed pine ringed with coffee stains and edged with burn marks from joints and cigarettes, laden with ashtrays and mugs and newspapers and magazines and books.

'Busy?' Max asked.

'Not especially.'

'Working on anything?'

'Burglary,' Plant said.

'Not your usual.'

'Someone had a computer stolen. Writing a history of up here, and had it all pinched.'

'What, Rock Richmond?'

'Why Rock Richmond?'

'Because he's been banging on about it for years, man. Writing his people's history of hippydom. Or oral history. Or whatever long lost, trendy term comes leaping out of his word-hoard.'

'Oh,' Plant said.

'Was I right?'

'Were you right about what?'

'Come on, man.'

'Client confidentiality.'

'So somebody burglarised Rock Richmond,' Max said, reflectively. 'Went off with the history of our times. *The Way*

We No Longer Live Now. They must have been desperate. What else did they take?'

'Nothing.'

'Poor sods. Can you imagine?'

'You hear anything about it?'

'Not a thing. You're the first to tell me.'

'Does it make any sense to you?'

'Not a lot. It's not like there'd be any market for it. Dear old Rock's day, if he ever had one, was long past before he ever moved up here.'

'I thought he always lived here.'

'No. No one's always lived here, man. Except the kooris and most of them were massacred.'

'How long's he been here?'

'A while. I'll give you that. Came up in the seventies some time. While the whole scene was bopping. Communes springing up like mushrooms. And lasting about as long.'

'Where did he come from?'

'Oh, I don't know. Down South. Sydney, Melbourne, Canberra, Adelaide. Somewhere like that.'

'How did you know he was writing a history?'

'Like I said, he's been going around talking about how it ought to be written. Asking people what they remember. Not a lot, in most cases. Most of them are totally wasted. But he was always going on about it. Even when he first came up. "This is an historic event. We should make sure we keep records. Woof, woof." You know what he's like. Or don't you?'

'I've met him.'

'Like a friendly puppy. Amiable enough. Very good on telling us all to keep records.'

'Was there anything to record?'

'There's always something to record.'

'Is there anything somebody mightn't want recorded?'

'Lots.'

'Like what?'

'Usual sexual carryings-on. All the dope stuff. People ripping off plantations. Crims moving in.'

'How did it all begin?'

'You don't know?'

'Not really.'

'You should ask Rock Richmond.'

'And he'd know?'

'Up to a point. He'd give you the official account. Whether it has any relation to the truth is something else again.'

'The official account?'

'Oh, he was always nosing around writing up reports on it. Nice work if you can get it. Paid for by the government or UNESCO or the World Bank or something. Didn't even have to hustle around getting it published.'

'So he wrote reports for the government.'

'For some official body or other. Somebody who could afford to fund them, anyway.'

'Were they published?'

'Not that I ever saw.'

'So why do you say they're the official account?'

'He was an official sort of person.'

'Is that so?'

'Compared with us.'

'In what way?'

'He was always well-connected. Seemed like it, anyway.'

'So what's the story?'

'Oh, man, this could take years.'

'A major research project.'

'I reckon.'

Max rolled up another smoke, and put the kettle on.

'Do you want the official history or the alternative history?'

'How about both?'

'The official history is that it all started with the alternative. The Aquarius Festival in 1973. Organised by the National Union of Students. Ten thousand New Age, anti-war, would-be hippies. Population of Nimbin before the festival, 250; population afterwards, 750. Increasing incrementally as they bred and more came and settled. The alternative history is a bit more complex. Though if you wanted to make it simple, you could say it was all about dope.'

People had been coming up north for years. Idyllic scenery. Great climate. Lots of small farms. Some were rich, beautiful people, some of them bought a traditional, middle-class beach house, some moved inland for a second home in the country. Economically they had the funds and the traditions of doing this. Some were weekenders, come down from Brisbane. Some were holiday homes, people come up from down south. Some were bought with retirement in mind. Some lay empty much of the year, some were occupied full-time. People who had retired, self-employed people. Arty folk, pottery and watercolours. Some were alternative, New Age. Some were communal settlements. People sharing an old farmhouse. People building on shared acreage – an old hundred-acre former dairy farm. Strictly illegal, but they did. So multiple occupancy developed. From Bellingen through the Northern Rivers up to Yandina. Some of this was cut-price individualism – shared acreage but enough room for privacy, individual houses. Some of it was communal – governing council meetings, shared cooking facilities, shared accommodation. Some were religious groups: Buddhists, Hare Krishnas. By the seventies there were all sorts of things going on. The official version was the Aquarius Festival started it all. But there were already things going on before that.

'Like what?' Plant asked.

'I reckon a few people had already figured it was perfect dope-growing country. That was what it was all about, basically. People who liked to smoke dope. Or sell it. That was the motivating factor.'

Surfies had been coming to Byron for years. Great waves. Great surfing. They were all into dope. Bringing it in from California and Hawaii. But importing was a risk, one way or another customs had to be dealt with. Domestic cultivation was a better alternative. The only problem was how to get cultivation in commercial quantities underway. It was not like Mexico or Thailand or Laos. There were no experienced local people around, keeping to themselves and specialising in growing it. The Murris that still survived here had never been into agriculture, being a basically nomadic people. There weren't any Chinese nationalist army divisions holed up in the hills. So maybe someone figured, what about bringing in some wetbacks? People who would plant it and water it and harvest it and keep quiet about it. But a massive importation of illegal Mexican aliens might have looked funny. So then some bright character says, Hippies. Hippies smoke the shit, hippies see themselves as an alternative society, opposed to the government. They'll keep to themselves. Easier to use than dairy farmers. Country people tend to be a bit set in their ways. In the end, of course, the country people got in on the act too. But to begin with they bring in the hippies. So how are you going to house them? Company barracks? No, communes. You set up communes. Cheap to set up, substandard accommodation, build their own, pitch a few tents.

'So who set up these communes?' Plant asked.

'Charismatic leader types.'

'Really?'

'Who else? Freaks. Every sort of freak. Religious freaks. New Age freaks. Power freaks. Environmental freaks. Anti-war freaks. Marie Antoinette freaks playing at shepherdesses. Military freaks.'

'Military?'

'Of course.'

'Why's that?'

'It was a time of war, man.'

'It's always a time of war.'

'Yes, but there was conscription. People had dodged the draft and run up here to hide out. Or they'd got called up and done their tour in Vietnam, developed a dope habit, and come up here and retired to the hills.'

'It could make an interesting history.'

'It certainly could,' Max said. 'I guess that was why Rock was writing it. Though whether anybody would want to read it today, I don't know.'

He poured the tea, and rolled another smoke.

'You need a deal?'

'Better take one.'

Max went out back and returned with a weighed ounce.

'What about Rock Richmond's wife?' Plant asked.

'I don't think she'd put it like that.'

'Like what?'

'I think she sort of feels Rock Richmond is her husband. He's the appendage. She's the power in the land.'

'Rock said she was a barrister.'

'Sure is.'

'Is there enough work around?'

'You'd better believe it.'

'Like what?'

'Oh, man, where've you been? Drugs, of course. What else? People getting busted for growing, supplying, possessing, driving under the influence of. The police fly the helicopters over and raid the plantations. She goes into court and says the plantations were not on her client's property but in adjacent designated national parkland anybody might have accessed. Or whatever. Illegal entry, search without warrant, undue force, and all the rest of it. Runs the case through for a year. Next year the helicopters fly over again. Every Christmas. New batch of arrests. Back to the courtroom. These are wealthy clients, man, it's worth a thousand bucks a plant. Money, money, money.'

'So Rock Richmond might have information on the drug culture.'

'He might,' Max said. 'If she tells him anything.'

'You're thinking of client confidentiality.'

'I'm thinking she's probably too busy to spend time talking to Rock Richmond.'

'Is that what you've heard? Even though she's married to him.'

'Recipe for a successful marriage, I would have thought,' Max said. 'She earns the megabucks, and he's the local icon that sits around the house looking decorative and dreams about being a best-selling writer.'

'Much like you,' Plant said.

'Well, I send the wife out to work but she doesn't bring in megabucks. Sadly.'

'But you have your dreams.'

'The thing about dope,' Max said, passing the joint across, 'is it cuts down on the dreaming.'

Chapter 4

Plant did the media calls. It was an easy enough job. Just sitting on the phone phoning round media contacts. Look out for stuff that might be in a certain style. What style is that? Indescribable, really, that was the problem, since he had to keep Rock Richmond's name out of it. And themes. Geriatric rock. Historic surf festivals. Alternative lifestyles. Communes.

'Doesn't sound the sort of thing we'd be interested in. Have you tried the Historical Feature editor?'

No one seemed terribly interested. Since he couldn't say who had been burgled there was no story in it; and since he couldn't tell them any details of the content he couldn't get anyone excited. It was a matter of doing the rounds, checking in, calling up, finding out who was holding which job now. A way of letting them know he was still in business. Of a sort. Research and investigation. Anyway, it was what Rock Richmond was paying him to do. So he did it. Then he visited Coolamon Scenic Drive again. He could have phoned. But he had spent long enough on the phone calling up features' editors and documentary producers. He liked the drive through the country lanes, the trees and fields washing past him, very calming with a morning smoke.

Rock Richmond answered the door. He ushered Plant in. Mrs Richmond was sitting on the couch with papers scattered around her, letters, files and things. No doubt things like transcripts and affidavits and stat. decs.

'Why don't you go to your room,' she said to Rock, like he was a child being banished for some misbehaviour. Perhaps he was.

'Good idea,' he said. 'This way,' he told Plant.

It was a small room at the end of the house but it had the same view. Rock Richmond stood at the window and looked at it, checking that it was indeed the same. A second set of books stood there dutifully in the bookcase. It still surprised Plant that there were as many as there were. They must have passed him by, year after year.

In the corner of the room the television flickered, BBC World with the sound off. On the magazine table the magazines were displayed. *Atlantic, New Yorker, Rolling Stone, Byron Shire Echo.* Wasn't Rock Richmond getting a bit old for *Rolling Stone?* Not that the Rolling Stones hadn't pretty well rolled over the hill by now. On the walls, framed photographs showed Rock Richmond with the celebrities of yesteryear. Writers. Politicians. School football teams. He seemed to have preserved them all. Rock in hippy garlands. Rock in radical chic combat gear. Rock with Princess Margaret, Allen Ginsberg, Germaine Greer, and various others Plant failed to recognise. He wondered if they were real photographs or cunning montages, Rock Richmond's once youthful features carefully inserted, their authenticity forever unquestioned, the celebrities all dead now or close to it.

'All done,' Plant said.

'Good man,' Rock Richmond said.

They stood looking out at the natural world.

'Another beautiful day,' Plant offered.

Rock Richmond blinked his eyes as if to sharpen his vision, and checked.

'As always,' he said. 'As always.'

Not strictly true, but upbeat. Even if the repetition gave it an elegiac note.

'Did anything turn up?' he asked.

Plant shook his head.

'No one's been offered anything, no one's heard of anything.'

'Well, that's good.'

'The material,' Plant said, 'do you want me to have a look through it?'

'I don't think so.'

'It might give some clue as to who stole it.'

'I can't see why.'

'Nor can I till I look at it.'

'No,' Rock Richmond said, 'no, I don't think that's the way to go.'

'Why not?'

'Ah well,' Rock Richmond said, wearily expansive, flopping down in an overstuffed leather chair and disappearing into it amidst the squeaks and creaks of the material. 'The thing is, some of it's, how shall I put it, some of it's not for public view.'

Plant wondered again if anything had actually been written. Was Richmond covering for the fact that he had nothing to show?

'Why's that?' Plant asked.

'Some of the files were commissioned work. It technically belongs to the people who commissioned it. I have to clear all that up before I go into print.'

'And who commissioned it?'

'Various agencies.'

'Literary agencies?'

'Government agencies.'

'Which ones?'

'Prime Minister's Department, Department of the Environment, Parks and Wildlife, Regional Development.'

'And they asked you to write reports.'

Rock Richmond nodded.

'Why?'

'Well why not?'

'Why were they concerned?'

'I'm not sure they were exactly concerned, as you put it. It was just a matter of interest.'

'Why?'

'The alternative was a phenomenon. I was here. Communes were springing up all over the place. It could have become quite big.'

'And the government wanted to control it?'

'No, no, not necessarily, not at all.'

'So why?'

'Environmental issues. Hospitals. Utilities. Planning. They had to consider introducing new legislation for multiple occupancy.'

'Hospitals?'

'If these became big settlements, or if there were a lot of them in certain areas, like there were up here, you'd need to ensure the social infrastructure was in place.'

'Like dole offices?'

'You're so cynical,' Rock Richmond said. 'Schools, first. If they all started breeding, as indeed they did, five years down the track you were going to have to make sure you had the schools for the kids. That sort of thing. Adequate health care facilities. Waste disposal.'

'And you were writing secret reports on all this.'

'Oh, not secret, for heaven's sake.'

'But you won't show them to me.'

'It's not that I won't, but I can't. It's a matter of copyright and ownership.'

'Uh-huh,' Plant said.

'Nothing secret about them. All above board.'

'And how many of them did you write?'

'Over the years?'

'Over the years.'

'Maybe half a dozen or so.'

'And why you?'

'Well,' Rock Richmond said. 'I had a name, you know, reporting on contemporary culture, working in television. They needed someone who was professional and who had a feel for the movement.'

'And you were living here? Or moved up here to write the reports?'

'Oh, a bit of both,' Rock Richmond said.

'So let me get this straight,' Plant said. 'You've written these half dozen governmental reports on the alternative or whatever? Or you're writing a book about the movement.'

'Both. I've got the reports and scenarios I wrote and I'll be drawing on them for the book.'

'Scenarios?'

'Yes.'

'Like film scripts?'

'No, scenarios. Futurology, you know.'

'Go on.'

'Future projections, global strategies. They used to be all the rage. Planning for the future by extrapolating current data.'

'And you were doing that.'

'When I was asked. It's just a different take on the data. Offering alternative outcomes. Best and worst case scenarios.'

'And all this was on file.'

'Yes.'

'And still is on your second set of back-ups.'

'Well, most of the reports pre-date computerisation. But I have the hard copies.'

'And they weren't stolen?'

'No.'

'Where are they?'

'Safe.'

'So writing this book is in effect just a matter of re-jigging the reports?'

'Oh no. Nothing's ever that easy. No, I'm going around interviewing survivors. Reflecting on it all. Taking an overview.'

'Survivors?'

'A lot didn't survive. They gave up, packed it in, went back to the city.'

'Survivors in that sense,' Plant said. 'I thought you meant a lot died.'

'Quite a lot did,' Rock Richmond said. 'Drugs, depression, accidents.'

'So does whoever pinched your stuff know you did these government reports and scenarios? Is that what they were after?'

'I've no idea. There's no reason anyone should know I'd written them. But there again, there was nothing top secret about them. I just didn't go around drawing attention to them.'

'You were discreet.'

'Sure.'

'But not necessarily undercover.'

'That's right.'

'And you don't think I should read these reports.'

'You'd have to get clearance.'

'And how would I do that?'

'No idea, to tell the truth.'

'So how are you going to get clearance to incorporate material from the reports into your book?'

'I may not do it like that. They'll serve to jog my memory. Raise the issues. But I probably won't take out material verbatim. They were reports, written in report style. They wouldn't really sit comfortably in a best-selling book.'

'It's going to be a best-seller?'

'You bet,' Rock Richmond said.

'Back in the charts.'

'With a bullet. This is the big one.'

A couple of hang-gliders came into view through the window. Rock Richmond gazed at them.

'If this material is so sensitive that I'd need clearance to read it, don't you think you should report its loss to the security services?'

'Don't know that I'd know how to.'

'You weren't doing reports for them?'

'Hardly.'

'You're sure of that?'

'Not directly, anyway.'

'But indirectly?'

'I suppose they might have accessed reports I did for the PM's Department or whatever. You never know.'

He smiled, reflectively. It seemed to give him a certain satisfaction. Rock Richmond, consultant to the secret state.

'But you don't think they need alerting?'

'I've reported it to the police. It's just a robbery.'

'But sensitive materials.'

'They're not that sensitive.'

'You won't let me see them.'

'Oh, it's not just that. I don't like showing people work in progress. I'm superstitious it will, you know, jinx it. And it always looks such a mess. You know how you want it to be, but until you've hammered it into shape you wouldn't want anyone seeing it.'

'Security people might find out better than I can who took it.'

'I don't especially want to know who took it. I just don't want my work turning up somewhere uncredited. And I'm in the middle of it. I'm still interviewing people. If the secret services or special branch go around asking questions, everyone will freeze up.'

'Why?'

'They'll assume I've been working for security.'

'Why would that worry them?'

'Because that's the sort of thing that worries them. They're all paranoid. They're all into anti-war protests and anti-logging and anti-development and anti-globalisation. Say No to Gas Seam Mining. They'd just freeze me out. The last thing we want is ASIO or the Feds nosing around.'

'If you say so.'

'I certainly do.'

Plant could see that he did. But he wasn't at all sure why.

'One other angle,' Plant said.

'Shoot.'

'Does the material you've written deal with dope?'

Rock Richmond gave a phlegmy laugh.

'It could hardly not, up here.'

'Is there sensitive material there? Someone who might not want to be named. Material you've picked up from your wife's legal practice?'

'My wife and I keep our professional careers entirely separate. I don't purloin her case notes and she ...' He stood at the window lost for an equivalent. 'She thinks what I write is pretty much shit anyway, so she doesn't have too much time for it.'

Chapter 5

She was still on the couch when they emerged, papers piled beside her. Affidavits, sworn legal statements, briefs, records of interview. She was in legal black. The sort of black you signed legal documents in. Ink-black. A day at home but still a working day. The country never sleeps. The law cannot afford to nod. Black jacket, black skirt, black stockings, white shirt.

She took off her glasses as they came in and directed her gaze in their direction. Plant wondered if she could see without glasses. Maybe she preferred not to see. Maybe it was a trick she practised in court to unnerve the recalcitrant witness. He could feel it unnerving him. Those black, baleful eyes, like a black Labrador, ready to devour anything. Everything. Plant wondered if she was short-sighted. Reliant on smell. Her nose twitched suggestively. Suggesting she was smell-reliant if nothing else. But there was something else, pervading the room. There was no denying the sexuality. And Plant was never one for denial. She was a decade or so younger than Rock. More like Plant's age. It didn't make him feel more at ease. He wondered if she was the second Mrs Richmond. Or had Rock's commitment to the alternative ensured he had married late?

'You boys finished having fun in the den, then?' she greeted them.

Rock Richmond looked pained but rearranged his features into a smile. Rapidly.

'Cat get your tongue?' she asked. 'Or was it secret men's business?'

'It wouldn't be secret if we told you,' Rock Richmond said.

'So tell me.'

'Plant's helping me with the robbery.'

'Burglary.'

'Whatever,' said Rock.

'There are significant legal differences,' she said. 'Not that I'd expect you to know.'

'No,' Rock agreed.

'So how are you helping my less than literate husband?' she asked Plant.

Rock Richmond put his arm round Plant's shoulder, protectively.

'To the best of my ability,' Plant said.

She gave him an appraising look. 'Is that saying much?'

'What you see is what you get,' Plant said.

'Is that so?'

There was a rasping sound of nylon on nylon as she slowly uncrossed her legs and rearranged them. Plant was unsure whether he found it erotic or not. His reading had suggested that he should. Maybe he didn't like artificial fibres. Or maybe it wasn't that that set his teeth on edge and sent shudders up his spine and set the back of his neck tingling. Maybe it was just fear. He knew he had a problem with strong women. Ambivalence, that was his problem.

'So are you going to get hubby's hobby back for him?'

'Hubby's hobby?'

'His history of oblivion. The brave new world that time forgot.'

'We'll give it a go.'

'We?' she said. 'Are you part of a team? Where are the rest of you?'

'Hidden resources.'

'You must come up and show me some time,' she said.

Rock Richmond cleared his throat, a long, withdrawing, shingled, sputum-laden surge of the surf.

'Yes, darling?' she turned to him.

'Nothing.'

'I thought you were about to pronounce.'

'Not me,' Rock Richmond said.

'Oh, lord, save me from weak silent men,' she said.

Plant tried to think of something to say, but everything had fled.

'So you plan on getting Rock's deathless prose back? Preserve it for immortality?'

'The first priority is to stop anyone else from using the material and selling it on.'

'Fat chance,' she said.

'Oh, we can do that,' Plant said.

'I'm sure,' she said. 'No problem. Who would sell it on, anyway? Who would want to buy it?'

Rock's pride was aroused. 'All sorts of people,' he suggested.

'Name two,' she said.

'It's a unique archival source.'

'Yeah, well, bottle it and sell it to put on meat pies.'

'My wife ...' said Rock.

'She has a name, as it happens, not just an outmoded patriarchal role designation.'

'My partner, Maggie,' said Rock, nodding obeisance at her, 'as I believe I mentioned, is not one of the biggest fans of my work.'

'You want a fan, go hire yourself a punkah wallah,' she said. She turned to Plant. 'My husband's income from writing is less than my outlay on incidentals. Forget print. You want money, you want audience share, go with the electronic media.'

'You speak as if you can just walk in there and do it,' said Rock, querulously.

'Why not?'

'It isn't that easy. There are a lot of people trying to get in there and a lot trying to keep them out and hang on to what they've got. It isn't as if I don't try.'

'Then you'll just have to try harder,' she said, 'won't you?'

Rock opened his mouth as if to complain again that it wasn't easy, but he said nothing. He gazed out at the view, across the ocean's curvature and down to Antarctica's icy wastes.

'You're too sensitive, you literary types. Weak bunch of wimps.'

Plant wondered if he was included amongst literary types. Why not, if she classed Rock Richmond as one? It was hard to know which was the most insulting, to be linked with Rock Richmond or to be described as a wimp. A weak wimp. Let alone literary. Well, everyone had a crack at a novel, once in a lifetime. Even Rock Richmond. Presumably as a barrister she chose her words with legalistic precision. Whichever way you looked at it, it wasn't flattering.

'They could be selling it to the electronic media,' said Rock. 'Using my name.'

'Anything's possible,' Plant agreed. 'People will do

anything.'

'It's unlikely,' Maggie said. 'What name?'

'It's a great data source for any medium,' Rock persisted.

'Probably all plagiarised from the internet anyway,' Maggie said.

'I say,' Rock said, 'come on.'

'Well, isn't everything these days? Or are you that seriously out of date you've been making it all up yourself?'

Rock returned to contemplating Antarctica.

'So how do you plan on getting it back? You going to offer a reward? Pay a ransom? Or call it paying for information received, like with art theft?'

They stood there silent.

'Well?' she asked.

'I think that's up to Rock,' Plant said.

'Then we might have to wait some time before we know,' she said. 'Slower than a glacier, our Rock of Ages.'

'I don't need them back,' said Rock. 'I just want to ensure no one else uses the material.'

She shook her head slowly from side to side.

'Looks like you've got yourself an easy job, Mr Plant,' she said.

'You can never tell,' Plant said.

'Well, if you can't, I'm sure Rock can't.'

Rock looked as if he might be able to tell a lot, or at least a bit, but thought better of it.

Chapter 6

Plant picked up some goat's milk cheese and matzos in Mullumbimby and a ripe avocado and a white apple cucumber from a roadside stall. He could have had a tomato from the stall too, but he decided he liked the cheese and avocado and cucumber just as they were, with some Kalamata olives he had in the fridge to sharpen the appetite. He took the rest of his fruit fermented, a bottle of supermarket red, a gentle Vin d'Oc Merlot. He put off thinking about Rock Richmond and his wife as long as he could, but somehow they insinuated themselves. He lived well, he congratulated himself; he might not be as wealthy as the Rock Richmonds, indeed he demonstrably wasn't; but he lived well. He sat in the sun and decided, I am happy, I live well, simply but well. Even as he congratulated himself, he knew it was the wrong thing to do. Never admit happiness, never concede contentment, never become self-satisfied: as soon as you do, the malign forces of the universe will do you down. Hubris, it was called.

That was when Fullalove arrived unexpected, unheralded, unannounced and unwelcome. He drove up the track through the bush in a Toyota ute and parked on the stretch of mown grass beside the verandah. Plant's lawn.

Plant had just rolled his after-lunch smoke. So smoking clogged up the arteries but it did not induce stress like unexpected visitors. It was stress that did the damage. The serious damage. Now he would need another couple of smokes to regain his shattered calm.

'You need to do something about security,' Fullalove said. 'Anybody could just drive in.'

'They just did,' Plant said.

Fullalove looked round rapidly, over his shoulder, over both shoulders, straight ahead and into the house.

'Where?'

'Right where you're standing.'

Fullalove sniffed. Sinuses clogged from the traffic fumes of a long drive, maybe. 'Oh, right,' he said. 'You had me worried there.'

Plant felt a brief moment of triumph, almost satisfaction.

'Put a gate up at least. And an infra-red sensor.'

'You good at putting up gates?' Plant asked.

'You're in the country, mate. That's what they do in the country, put up gates, put in fencing posts. Anyone could do it.'

'They haven't.'

'You've got to approach them in the right way,' Fullalove said. 'Offer them a slab of beer.'

'Feel free,' Plant said.

Fullalove unhooked the tarpaulin over the ute tray and took out a couple of suitcases.

'You've come to stay?' Plant inquired.

'Just till things blow over,' Fullalove said. 'That all right?' he asked. Rhetorically, really. How could Plant say no?

He took out a couple more packages, cardboard boxes stuffed with books and magazines and papers.

'Travelling light,' Plant said.

'Always do.'

'That's all your earthly possessions?' Plant asked. Apprehensively. It could mean Fullalove was planning to move in.

'Research,' Fullalove said.

'What on?'

'Oh, this and that,' Fullalove said. 'This and that.'

'What's with the ute?' Plant asked.

'Perfect surveillance vehicle.'

'Is that so?'

'No one notices a ute parked in the street. They assume it's just a tradesman. Invisible.'

'You'll get a bit hot sitting in a ute cab up here,' Plant said. 'You should've got one with a double cab. Otherwise you're going to have to sit there with the engine running to run the air-conditioning.'

'Open the windows, easy.'

'Then they'll see you sitting there.'

'I might get a fibreglass canopy over the back.'

'You should've got one with a high wheel-base for up here. For when the creeks get flooded.'

'Anything else?' Fullalove said.

'Yes, you need a dog. No ute's complete without a dog tied up in the back barking at the other vehicles on the road.'

'What are friends for?' Fullalove asked.

'So who's under surveillance?'

'Just an investment for the future.'

'You ever done any surveillance?'

'You mean am I a common or garden snoop like you? No. But am I an investigative journalist?'

'No,' Plant said.

'You'll see,' Fullalove said.

'How did you find me?' Plant asked, his country retreat invaded, the address he had carefully given to no one discovered.

'I wasn't a top reporter for nothing,' Fullalove said.

'You never told me the salary.'

'These things are confidential.'

'So was my address,' Plant said. 'How did you find it out?'

'Had your phone number, didn't I? You got a landline, you've got an address. You got an address, all you need is to look at a map. Then you get in a car and drive.'

'Why me?' Plant asked.

'Don't know too many people in the sticks,' Fullalove said. 'Not my scene.'

'So why have you come?'

'Change of venue,' Fullalove said. 'Get away from the usual haunts. Thought I'd keep a low profile for a while.'

'How long a while?'

'As long as it takes,' Fullalove said.

'So what's this all about?'

'I'm making a comeback.'

'A comeback? I thought you said you were running away.'

'Dialectics, mate.'

'Dialectics?'

'Thesis and antithesis. Dialectics and subterfuge.'

Fullalove sat on the verandah and lit up. Plant passed him across an ashtray.

'What's this?' Fullalove asked.

'An ashtray.'

'An ashtray? Looks like an old shell to me.'

'It is.'

'Don't you have any proper ashtrays?'

'It is a proper ashtray.'

'Business bad up here, is it? Can't afford ashtrays.'

'They're natural,' Plant said.

Fullalove looked at him balefully.

'Organic. Environmental. Ecological,' Plant added. 'Live off the land.'

Fullalove surveyed the spreading view. Bush. More bush. Gums, camphor laurels, more gums, more camphor laurels.

'Can't see you making much of a living living off of this lot.'

'I like it like this.'

'Sure,' Fullalove said. 'Live off the land, live off the sea. Catching fish I can understand. Shells for ashtrays I can't.'

'It's traditional,' Plant added. 'Beach houses always have shell ashtrays.'

'Traditional?' Fullalove said. 'You become a conservative now you've moved up here? Can't see any beach, either.'

'You want to go there?'

'And collect shells?'

'Sure,' Plant said. 'It depends on what the currents are. Different times you get different sorts of shells. Last week I got half a dozen cowries and a sea urchin.'

Fullalove looked at him in sincere amazement.

'Man, I can't believe what I'm hearing.'

But he put the shell beside his chair and scattered ash in a circle around it.

'Need a bigger shell,' he said. 'One of those man-eating clams.'

'What's this thing in the shower?' Fullalove called out.

'What thing?'

'This sponge thing.'

'It's a sponge.'

'Funny looking sponge.'

'It's a natural sponge.'

Fullalove resumed the conversation when he emerged, wrapped in towels, dripping water across the sea-grass matting, the hair of his head and hairy heels damp and tangled like seaweed.

'What do you mean, natural?' he asked.

'Like from nature.'

'Where did you buy it?'

'I didn't.'

'Some stay-overnight chick left it behind?'

'I picked it up on the beach.'

'You what?' Fullalove said. He stood there aghast, dripping drops like a shaking dog.

'I found it on the beach.'

'Shit, man, it could be poisonous.'

'It's a sponge.'

'How do you know there aren't poisonous sponges?'

'I guess we'll find out,' Plant said.

'It could have poison sacs deep down inside. Like stonefish poison. Or blowfish.'

'If you turn into a zombie I'll keep you to work the land,' Plant said.

'How do you know it hasn't got AIDS?'

'How could it?'

'Maybe somebody already used it. Threw it off a yacht because it was contaminated.'

Plant pondered.

'You don't know, do you?' Fullalove said. 'You don't know anything about it. It could be fucking lethal.'

'I doubt it,' Plant said.

But the damage had been done. Plant looked at it the next time he showered and left it sitting there in the soap tray. Maybe somebody had used it and thrown it overboard. Anyway, Fullalove had certainly used it. He looked at it again. He turned off the shower and went out for an environmentally-unfriendly plastic bag from the kitchen and put the sponge and the soap into it and dumped them in the garbage. And then went back and washed his hands. Vigorously.

'I was doing a story,' Fullalove said.

'You're writing fiction now?'

'I might,' Fullalove said. 'Could be the way to go.'

'Which way is that?'

'To a long and happy life,' Fullalove said. 'Long, anyway. Rather than violent curtailment. I might just do it as fiction.'

'Do what?'

'What I've been working on.'

'Which is?'

'Oh, research and investigation, you know. Your sort of thing.'

Yes, Plant knew. It was on his business card. Research assistance, investigative reporting. Though you could hardly call it a business card. Not without exaggeration. More a quiet understated plea for employment. Generally unheard.

'I was big once,' Fullalove said.

'You've lost weight.'

'Big,' Fullalove said. Looking at the entertainment guide. 'All these names from pre-history you thought were dead. They probably are. Half the time they're impersonations. Like Elvis.'

He read through the billings, avidly.

'Too young to die, too fat to live.'

'You're not fat,' Plant said.

'Big, not fat,' Fullalove said. 'I was a name to conjure with. And I lost it all. A media star. Mega-star.'

'When was that?' Plant asked.

'No one remembers, see,' Fullalove said. 'Like all these rock-n-rollers. No one remembers them. It comes to everybody. Here are all these mega names from the past playing in bowling clubs and country pubs and community halls. Forgotten but not gone. Tragic, really.'

He pored over the gig guide.

'Tragic,' he repeated with satisfaction. 'It comes to everybody.'

He went back to the television and surfed through the channels.

'Of course the mistake is,' he said, 'when you've been done over, when you've been big and you've been done down and are in the gutter, the mistake is to start identifying with other victims. Reading all about the martyred. It's just an indulgence, wallowing in grief and self-pity. When you should be out there observing the rich and successful and modelling yourself on them. Forget the failures. Screw the victims. Otherwise you'll stay as one.'

'Is that so,' Plant said.

'It certainly is,' Fullalove said.

Chapter 7

Fullalove contemplated the night sky in unfeigned terror. *Ces espaces infinis m'effraie.* He sat out on the verandah with a joint in a trembling hand, looking up at the Milky Way in anxious apprehension, like a stray cat marauding for food and expecting something to reach down and strike him.

'I don't know how you can stand it,' he said.

'Stand what?'

'Living out here. With all those stars. One thing about the city, at least you never see them. The lights block them all out.'

'I rather like them,' Plant said.

'Doesn't it make you feel ...' Fullalove reached for the word, gesturing with the joint through the night air. 'Unimportant?' he hazarded.

'We are unimportant.'

'Not me,' Fullalove said. 'I was big once. And I'm going to be big again.'

'Eat some more of this,' Plant said, passing across the cherry strudel.

'You know what I mean,' Fullalove said.

'Your name up in lights, blocking out the stars.'

'Exactly,' Fullalove said.

Appeased, he sliced off some strudel.

'Back where I belong.'

'And how are you going to do that. Carbohydrates apart.'

'This story I'm working on,' Fullalove said. 'Unless it

gets me killed first. It'll make me or break me.'

'I wonder which.'

'You don't have to wonder,' Fullalove said. 'You can be there.'

'I'm not sure I want to be.'

'Where's your ambition?'

'Gone,' Plant said.

'Where's your sense of adventure?'

'Never had much.'

'So what you going to do the rest of your life?'

'Contemplate the stars,' Plant said.

'Bugger that,' Fullalove said. 'The only star I'm going to contemplate is myself.' He sucked on the joint. 'A mega star,' he said. 'That's what I'm going to be when I've got this story.'

'Unless it gets you killed first.'

'Yes, well,' Fullalove said. 'There is that. But that's the risk you take.'

'Not for me,' Plant said.

'Too late, mate,' Fullalove said.

'What do you mean?'

'Once they find out I'm staying here and I've been talking to you, you'll be on the list too.'

'If they find out.'

'Oh, they'll find out,' Fullalove said.

Plant felt something of Fullalove's frisson of fear seize him. He looked up at the stars in attempt to calm down. He took a drag on the remains of the joint and burned his lips and fingers.

'Can you tell me what this is all about?' Plant asked.

'No.'

'What do you mean, no?'

'No can do,' Fullalove said.

'What's that supposed to mean?' Plant asked.

'Need to know principle,' Fullalove said. 'Best you know nothing.'

'I see,' Plant said.

'Good.'

Fullalove was insistent about getting a gate.

'I can't sleep at night.'

'Is that so?'

'I need security.'

'Another blanket?'

'Just a gate.'

'Maybe you should move up the Gold Coast. Rent an apartment. One of those with closed-circuit TV and security doors.'

'No, I'm comfortable here.'

Plant registered defeat. He had been doing his best to discomfort Fullalove. But Fullalove's concept of comfort was a unique thing. He survived on the minimal. There seemed no way to make him uncomfortable enough to want to move on. He had dug in and had no intention of going.

'Doesn't need to be an expensive gate. Just something to stop villains driving up to the house.'

'Yes,' Plant said. 'I can see the appeal.'

Why hadn't he done it before? Before Fullalove had driven up.

'Can't you get onto it?'

'Why can't you?'

'I'm keeping a low profile,' Fullalove said, stretching out on the recliner chair and ashing the verandah. 'I go around asking about gates, someone's going to wonder. Who's this cove we've never seen before? Why's he asking about gates? People talk. Word gets round. And then, pow.'

'Pow?'

'Too right,' Fullalove said. 'Pow, wham, bam.'

'Ah,' Plant said. 'Pow, wham, bam.'

Plant pulled up down the road and talked to the banana farmer.

'Where would I get a gate?'

'A gate?'

'To put across the driveway there.'

'Across the driveway?'

'Where would I go to get one?'

'I can get you a gate,' the farmer said.

'I want to pay for it,' Plant said.

'I can get you a good price.'

'Really? Where from?'

'From the bloke we get our gates from.'

'Could you?'

'No problem.'

'Can you get me a price?'

'I can get you a good price.'

'How much, about?'

'Oh.' He scratched his jaw. 'I'll have a look next time I'm out there.'

'Who puts up gates round here?'

'Who puts up gates?'

'Yes.'

'Oh,' he said, reflectively. 'I can put a gate.'

'No, I'm happy to pay for it.'

'I can put up a gate,' he said again. 'There's a couple of posts there, aren't there?'

'I don't know. I don't think so.'

'I've seen them there.'

'Really? I've never noticed.'

'Should be,' the farmer said. 'I'll measure them up. Just a gate?'

'Just a gate.'

'No problem.'

'If you could let me know the price.'

'No worries.'

Fullalove drove off on his morning compulsion to buy the daily papers, having exhausted the satellite news channels. Plant rolled himself a smoke and sat out on the verandah. Within minutes Fullalove was back, reversing up the driveway in an erratic zigzag, slicing into the lawn. He ran out of the ute, the door left hanging open. As close to a run that Plant had seen Fullalove achieve.

'They've shut us in,' Fullalove said.

Plant palmed the joint.

'They've barricaded the track. We can't get out.'

'Who have?'

'Best you don't know,' Fullalove said.

'How do you know?'

'I know these things,' Fullalove said.

'So what have they done?'

'They've blocked the exit. We're trapped in here.'

Plant walked down the avenue of camphor laurels and gums. Cautiously. Pigeons trampled in the high branches. Kookaburras cackled. Magpies warbled. Somewhere in the distance a power saw droned.

Across the track a structure of metal bars blocked the way. Plant felt his heart pound, a sinking plunge of anxiety convulsed his stomach. He kept walking, between the banks of moss-encrusted red soil and the delicate ferns. The ends of the structure were obscured by bushes and branches, but as he approached closer it revealed itself as a gate. A loose loop of wire kept it in position, hooked over the gatepost Plant had never noticed. Hinges had been nailed into the post the other side of the track.

From down the road the banana farmer's old International truck made its stately way into view. It pulled up.

'Give you a fright, did I?' the farmer grinned.

'It did a bit,' Plant conceded.

'Thought you'd been locked in, did you?'

'For a few anxious moments,' Plant said.

'Thought you might,' the farmer said.

'What do I owe you?' Plant asked.

The farmer shrugged.

'It'll be on the account.'

'About how much?'

'Won't know till the end of the month.'

'Well, let me know when you know how much it is.'

The farmer grinned.

'And thanks a lot,' Plant said. 'It was very kind of you.'

'Thought it might give you a fright,' the farmer said, happily.

Chapter 8

Fullalove looked apprehensively at the natural world. He sat on the verandah and peered. Sometimes he lay on the recliner chair and peered. As far as could be ascertained nothing peered back. Nature displayed its grand indifference.

'Where's the boundary fence?'

'There isn't a fence,' Plant said.

'What do you mean, there isn't a fence?'

'Why would I want a fence? It's just bush. I'm not running any stock.'

'So how do you keep people out?'

'Apart from you there haven't been any people to keep out. Just wallabies and snakes.'

'Snakes,' Fullalove said.

'Toads, spiders, goannas,' Plant said.

'I don't know how you stand it.'

'I love it.'

Fullalove grunted.

'So where's the boundary line?'

'You want to patrol it?'

'It wouldn't be a bad idea,' Fullalove said. 'Now we've got the gate up.'

Plant equipped him with gumboots and insect repellent and pointed him away from the house.

'What about the snakes?' Fullalove asked.

'They'll run away when they feel the vibrations of your feet.'

'What if they don't?'

'Find yourself a forked stick,' Plant said.

'Where would I do that?'

'Beneath the camphor laurels. The branches fall down all the time.'

'What if one falls on me?'

'Don't even think about it,' Plant said. 'If it's a big one you'll never know anything about it.'

'You got a hat?'

'A hat won't help. You need a helmet.'

Fullalove went to the ute and took out a hard hat from beneath the tarpaulin.

'Part of your surveillance cover?' Plant asked.

But Fullalove had already set off on patrol. Down to the front gate. Back up through the bush along the creek, following a line that might have been the boundary.

'You want to set some man-traps?' Plant asked when he returned.

'Wouldn't be a bad idea. You got some?'

'No.'

'Where can you get them?'

'I think they're probably illegal,' Plant said.

'Lots of things are. Doesn't mean you can't get them. Why don't you ask that banana farmer of yours?'

'Sure,' Plant said, insincerely, wearily.

'What you need are those surveillance border towers like they used to have in Eastern Europe. Probably still do. They wouldn't be hard to build.'

'Feel free,' Plant said.

'Like fire-watching towers.'

'I know the sort.'

'What do you reckon to building a couple?'

'Feel free.'

'Can you give us a hand?'

'No.'

'Why not?'

'I'm not a builder.'

'Nor am I,' Fullalove said.

'There you are then.'

'What about that farmer friend of yours? Maybe he'd build one.'

'Maybe.'

'There must be plans on the internet.'

Plant resigned the computer to him. At least it occupied him. Took him away from the satellite news channels. He went outside and sat on the verandah with a smoke while Fullalove irradiated himself before the computer screen.

'How long, how long?' he asked himself. 'When will this be taken from me?'

It was like a state of siege. Fullalove inviting himself to stay in the country, the utter inner urbanite, fleeing from villains, making himself scarce, though not scarce for Plant. Fullalove peering up at any noise. The chase of the electricity meter-reader's van down the lane to get an approved padlock for the gate, one that could be opened by the emergency services and the electricity meter-readers. Plant could envisage ambulances, forensic scientists, fire engines all hurtling up, and the drug squad combing through the lantana, looking for his seedlings. Fullalove, the man who came to dinner. Like Cocteau, staying for ever. And watching the news channels endlessly, Sky, Sky London, BBC World, CNN, Fox, ABC Australia, ABC US, CBS, SBS, PBS, Deutsche Welle, Al Jazeera. And when they palled turning to the finance news, CNBC, Bloomberg,

Sky Business Channel, or the Weather channel. With a documentary about Hitler or the Kennedy assassinations on the History channel for variety. Plant retreated to his hammock. Ticks fell off the trees it was attached to and burrowed into his flesh. He retreated back indoors, Fullalove sitting there in his unmistakably urban clothes, dark, heavy fabrics, sticking to him with sweat, shirt unbuttoned, stomach protruding, pallid flesh. Once in a while he lumbered up and looked through the kitchen and fridge for things Plant did not have like milk, coffee, Vegemite, peanut butter, chocolate, Nutella, sausages, bacon, crumpets. He mocked the offers of dandelion coffee, peppermint tea, carob.

While Fullalove was out on patrol Plant took the opportunity to air the room he had occupied. Open the windows to their widest extremity. The stale smell of sweat and cigarette smoke, dope, red wine, old clothes, newspapers, all hung there reluctant to disperse. It possessed the space like a cluster of disincarnate entities imported from the inner city. Plant gathered up the accreted cups and glasses and ashtrays, emptied and washed them. But each day they had been drawn back in. He restrained himself from picking up the clothes from the floor. There were limits to how far he would play mother. He restrained himself from directing Fullalove to the washing machine. It was like a home invasion. Fullalove may have felt under threat of attack. But for Plant, the attack had already occurred. Now he was held hostage. He did not even like to leave the house alone for any length of time. He dreaded what Fullalove might do to the place, left there on his own. He checked through the insurance policy to make sure he was covered for fire, flood and storm. He made a point of insisting Fullalove came with him when they went out for supplies.

Plant placed his Akubra hat on the back window ledge of the car. Protection. Like his country shirt and his new tweed jacket. Like the car, too. A no longer late model Hyundai Accent. As Fullalove might concede, a good surveillance vehicle. Something not to stand out. Did Plant lust after a Jaguar or an Aston-Martin or a Maserati? Only sometimes. For that matter, why not a classic Daimler or a Bentley tourer in British racing green or a Lagonda or an Hispano-Suiza? Or even a Morgan, as long as it wasn't the old three-wheeler Morgan runabout, that would take things into the realms of the ridiculous, like a Reliant. But apart from their unattainability, they would all be too noticeable. He preferred to aim for a condition of unnoticeability. And not just as part of the job. That was why he carried the hat. Even wore it. But mainly carried it in the car. So he would look like a boring old banana farmer from the sticks rather than a substance abuser. He did not want to be stopped for driving too slowly. He did not want to encourage the taking of blood and saliva samples. But the subterfuge was ruined by Fullalove's urban ghetto look in the passenger seat. It shrieked drugs. Up here, anyway. Fullalove was ruining it all, filling the ashtray with cannabis ash, scattering it over the seat fabric, breathing out his foetid breath to condense on the windscreen.

'Just sit down low in the seat and pull a hat over your eyes.'

Fullalove stretched the passenger seat back to its fullest and inserted his head inside his hard hat.

It was like being possessed by a space creature. Something that had come down from the stars one night as Plant had sat out there on the verandah. Invaded by aliens. One alien. With the force of Legion.

Chapter 9

The days were warm but at Plant's hideaway in the foothills the evenings were cold enough for a fire. The early mornings were cold enough, too, but lighting a fire in the morning was something Plant had been brought up to believe was somehow immoral, like reading a novel in the morning, or watching daytime movies on television, or having a drink before noon. It had not been a counter-cultural, alternative childhood. More one of vigorous Puritanism and the Protestant work ethic. The idea was you bustled around being busy in the morning, washing up, sawing wood, sweeping and scrubbing, mowing lawns, planting potatoes, and that kept you warm. Plant did none of it. Instead he put on his new tweed jacket. He had tired of the blue blazer number. He wanted rural. When he went out doing his shopping in Murwillumbah or Mullumbimby he wanted to look as if he had just come in from the bush, in the styles of yesteryear, when values were old and true. Even the 1950s looked more liberal, more progressive, more committed to free speech and open debate than the twenty-first century. It was the sort of jacket he could wear to buy a sultana cake or an afternoon tea bun: let alone a custard tart or an apple pie.

'Shit man,' Fullalove said, 'you really are in Tweed. Literally. Got the jacket to match the shire.'

He gave a series of laughs that broke up into coughs and hawking and spitting.

He reached out and fingered it.

'Where's the leather patches?'

'You only put patches on when the elbows have worn through.'

'No kidding. Sure you can't buy them with leather patches?'

'You can, in Melbourne. But they're inauthentic.'

'Is that so? What about leather strips round the cuffs?'

'That's if they start to fray.'

'All these codes and conventions,' Fullalove said. 'Never knew you were such an authority on sumptuary laws.'

Plant did not need Fullalove's urban derision. Let alone urban ignorance. It wasn't in fact a tweed jacket. It was labelled European cloth. It could have come from anywhere, Italy, Poland, Slovenia. It was not as heavy as Harris Tweed. And it was very multicoloured. 'It will match with everything,' the salesman had assured him, 'whatever colour, it will be there.' Sometimes wearing it Plant felt like a radiant autumn in the northern hemisphere.

Outside the remorseless hooting bird began its remorseless hooting.

'You all dressed up for a case?'

'I'm dressed up for warmth.'

'You got any cases?'

'Yes and no,' Plant said.

'Well, that's an interesting answer. Who is it?'

'Client confidentiality,' Plant said.

'You know me,' Fullalove said.

'All too well,'

'Need some help on it?'

'Not really.'

'Want to tell me about it?'

'Not especially.'

'Just to fill up the idle hours,' Fullalove said. 'Keep my mind from vegetating in the rural idiocy. I might be able to give you a pointer or two.'

Plant told him. It was more or less over, anyway. The media had been warned. As for who might have done the burglary, Rock Richmond had discouraged any active investigation. It was now just a matter of keeping an ear to the ground in case anything turned up. Fullalove's ears were closer to the ground than most people's. There seemed no reason not to make use of him. As far as Plant could see, there was nothing else Fullalove would be any use for.

'Rock Richmond,' Fullalove said. 'Is he still alive?'

'Prosperous,' Plant said.

'He always was prosperous,' Fullalove said.

'Always?'

'Sure. You don't think he could make a living off the stuff he wrote, do you? Wealthy family. Had to be. Squattocracy. That's how he got in. No other way. That's why they gave him space. Used to write these piddling pieces about youth culture. That's what they used to call it, youth culture. So he got by on writing what were effectively fillers.'

Fullalove's resentment was palpable. His tone veered between contempt and envy, rage and unfulfilled desire.

'I thought he was one of the New Journalists,' Plant said.

'Ah, those old New Journalists. Back when they were new, before they were mercifully forgotten. Half a dozen zippy words for the opening paragraph, and then the same old stuff every journalist hacked out. You know. "Hip, hip, yippee! The central target of the five-year plan remains in sight of being reached, government sources stated last week in Canberra." But he always had the glitzy pop vocabulary for the opening pars. Fast fading as it was.'

'A lot of people wrote like that then,' Plant said.

'Is that so?'

'Everyone sprinkled the odd "Triparoo!" and "Cool, man!" and "What a blast!" through their stuff.'

'Not everyone. And certainly not I,' Fullalove said, with scrupulous regard for grammar.

'Ah well, fashions change.'

'Nothing to do with fashion,' Fullalove said. 'He was going to be there whatever the fashion. He had the right connections, they fixed him up, gave him the space. A sort of journalistic remittance man.'

'How do you know that?' Plant asked.

'I just do. It's obvious. You can just assume it.'

'And what you just assume is true.'

'Unless proved otherwise.'

'And was it?'

'Was it what?'

'Proved otherwise.'

'No idea.'

'But you just assume it anyway.'

'Journalistic ethics.'

'Aren't you being unfair?'

'All's fair in journalism and war. Those guys had it easy. If I were to go along and say, "You want some stories on the youth culture, I can cover it, drugs, music, sex, you name it," they'd just say, "Piss off, this is a serious paper." But because he had his connections they'd run his ramblings in the colour magazine or the lifestyle pages. Meant they didn't have to worry about hiring anyone serious who might end up saying something. The ground was covered.

Safe pair of hands.'

'You don't approve,' Plant said.

'Too right I don't approve,' Fullalove said, 'and I'll tell you why. First of all, he just got the job through connections.'

'Which you don't happen to have.'

'Which I don't happen to have. Nor, let me add, do you as far as I can see.'

Plant shrugged. He was not sure whether that was a matter of praise or blame. Mainly Fullalove seemed to be into blame at the moment.

'And secondly,' Fullalove said, 'I don't approve because I happen to believe in newspapers. Or used to. I happen to believe they have a duty to inform. Readers are entitled to good, informed writing. Which Rock Richmond certainly never gave them. Trivialisation, that's what he specialised in.'

'Maybe that was what the managements wanted.'

'Of course it was,' Fullalove said. 'That's why I don't approve. It's your duty as a journalist to resist dumbing down. You've got to stand up to management.'

'As demonstrated in your career.'

'Yes,' Fullalove said.

'Which is why you have no career.'

'I intend to make a comeback.'

'So does Rock Richmond.'

'Spare us.'

'Somebody seems to be trying to,' Plant said. 'They stole his computer.'

'Good on 'em,' Fullalove said. 'Whoever they are. Not that there'd be anything worth stealing. What is he supposed to have been writing about?'

'The alternative culture.'

'Right up to the minute as ever.'

'Well, he was writing it as a history, not journalism.'

'You're in his inner confidence?'

'I don't know about that. But he hired me.'

'To get his ramblings back.'

'No.'

'That's something. What did he want?'

'He wanted me to make sure no one else published the stuff.'

Fullalove laughed.

'That will be the day. Somebody stealing Rock Richmond's copy to try and flog it. What a joke. What a shock when they realise what they've got. Unpublishable, I can assure you. Not that that ever stopped it from being published.'

'So he wasn't that bad.'

'Depends on what you see as good.'

'So why would they have stolen his files if he's as bad as you say?'

'Oh, he's as bad as I say,' Fullalove assured him. 'Worse. I guess they made a serious mistake. Must have been amateurs.'

'It was a professional job. A quick in and out, nothing else taken.'

'Just the computer?'

'And the back-up. All the other electronic gear, and there was some, the latest, they didn't touch.'

'So they knew what they wanted.'

'Looks like it.'

'Even though we know no one would want it.'

'Do we?'

'I do.'

'Perhaps he turned up something. He said he had a scoop. It was going to be a best-seller.'

'Never.'

'That's what he said.'

'I'm sure. But it wouldn't have been.'

'You don't think he turned up something. Not even accidentally? Unaware?'

'He's more likely to bury things than turn them up. He's a four-square establishment boy.'

'So maybe it was something he was trying to bury.'

'I give you this,' Fullalove said. 'It's certainly a mystery. I mean, if someone really wanted to know what he was writing, they would just hack in there with some spyware. So it looks like this was also a warning to kind of stop writing what he was writing. Theft as message.'

'You reckon stealing his computer and his back-up was meant to stop him working on the project?'

'What else?'

'What if he doesn't?'

'He's a well-brought-up old boy. He can take a hint.'

'What if he's determined?'

'They know him. He's one of them. They know he isn't that determined. He might think he is, but he'll probably never get it back together. Not being one of your dynamic high flyers these days. They'd have figured he'll just take the easy way out and leave it.'

'But he hasn't.'

'I guess they underestimated the lure of fame.'

'Or the satisfactions of a job well done.'

'Could be,' Fullalove said. 'But I'll settle for the lure of fame.'

Chapter 10

Later Plant wondered whether Fullalove's insistence that Rock Richmond could know nothing was a devious interrogation trick. Instead of asking what Richmond had told him and what Plant had discovered, he insisted there couldn't be anything. So that instead of clamming up in the face of inquiries, Plant found himself revealing the details in order to insist that there was something of substance there. Revealing that Richmond was determined to carry on with the project. But that was later, when he had occasion to reflect.

Immediately, he found himself resisting Fullalove's jealous doubts and embittered scepticism and insisting there must be something in Rock Richmond's researches or reports.

'These reports he wrote,' Plant said, 'what do you reckon about them?'

'Old stuff.'

'But who were they really for? Why did they want them?'

'Search me.'

'Doesn't it suggest the alternative was being monitored?'

'Of course it was being monitored. Everything's monitored. You can't have a church or a trade union or a magazine of a community group without it being monitored. You're monitored on the freeway and in the shopping mall and outside the ATM and passing the airport and at the gas station. They'd have had sources inside all the communes. Drug squad, feds, whatever it takes.'

'But were Rock Richmond's reports part of the monitoring?'

'Could be,' Fullalove said. 'Though why would they bother if they had their people inside?'

'If they had people inside.'

'Of course they did. They had an ASIO informer at Nimbin from the very beginning. He's even admitted it. They were looking for draft dodgers and anti-war activists and runaways, they were bound to keep those places under surveillance. Communes, crash pads, drop-in centres.'

'So maybe Rock Richmond was doing something else?'

'Never struck me he was ever doing anything.'

'He assured me he'd got revelations. World-shattering stuff.'

'Is that what he said?'

'World-shattering stuff? Yes.'

'And did you ask him what it was?'

'I did.'

'And did he tell you?'

'No. He said it was under wraps till publication. He didn't want any word getting out.'

'Delusions of grandeur,' Fullalove said.

'Maybe. But he was burgled.'

'So he says.'

'Though the reports weren't stolen. They're in hard copy, they weren't on the computer.'

'Well, if it was a government job, they wouldn't need to steal the reports because they'd have them already. So if it's anything at all, it's something new. Something he didn't put in the reports. Something he only just discovered or realised the significance of.'

'Maybe.'

'I'll think about it. If it didn't involve Rock Richmond I might take it seriously. But with him I find it hard to. Think what I could have done with his connections. The guy's wired and all he writes is shit.'

'Maybe that's the point.'

'Of course it is,' Fullalove snarled. 'It doesn't make it any better, though.'

'I guess not.'

'You may be happy with your mediocre life out in the sticks,' Fullalove said. 'But me, I refuse to settle for this.'

'You want Rock Richmond's riches and scenic view.'

'Not especially.'

'Fame, wealth and glamour?'

'I wouldn't refuse. I tell you, man, I couldn't live like you do with all this weird stuff. Shells. Sponges. Fir cones. What's with the fir cones?'

Along the verandah beside the bags of firewood were four wine boxes filled with fir cones Plant had collected.

'This whole place is a fire-trap. It looks like a mad house, Plant. You're going feral. You think you're a born-again hippy. You just need some arsonist coming round and the whole lot would go up whoosh ...'

'The point of the fir cones,' Plant said, 'is exactly that; going up whoosh.'

'Is that so? You got a spot of self-immolation in mind?'

'They're natural fire-lighters. Say there's a power failure. Which happens all the time and now we're promised more. A long-term one. No oil. An atomic explosion. No electricity. You're dependent on fires. But lighting fires isn't just a matter of striking a match. Sometimes they won't light. The twigs on the ground are all damp. So what do you do? You stockpile fir cones, that's what you do. I collect them along the road. And they're free. Not like buying firelighters.'

'Spare me,' Fullalove said. 'You've turned into a mountain man. And I suppose fir cones are more environmentally friendly than firelighters, too. Is this the sort of thing Rock Richmond's history of the alternative was going to be about? Shell ashtrays and poisonous sponges and fir cones.' He stopped, considered the portents. 'I think it was,' he concluded. 'No wonder they stole his computer. Anything to stop this sort of thing.'

'Are you going to the Writers' Festival?' Fullalove asked.

'Why would I do that?'

'You given up writing?'

Plant shrugged. Maybe he had. Or maybe writing had given him up. Or maybe he was just resting.

'You planning on going?' he asked Fullalove. 'You've become a writer now?'

'I always was.'

'Always?'

'In my heart,' Fullalove said.

'Your what?'

'Heart.'

'That's what I thought you said.'

'I have a heart,' Fullalove said.

'I suppose so.'

Fullalove placed his hand against where it might have been.

'And that's where your literary talent hides itself?'

'I was a journalist.'

'So was I,' Plant said.

'Freelancing for the press doesn't make you a journalist,' Fullalove said.

'Everyone's freelance now, pretty well.'

'Now, maybe. But I was on staff.'

'Till you were sacked,' Plant pointed out.

'Let go,' Fullalove corrected. 'Whereas I don't recall that you were ever taken on.'

'On the other hand,' Plant pointed out, 'I was a novelist.'

'A ghost novelist.'

'You want to hire me to ghost-write your new project, is that why you're here? You're writing a novel?'

'I might let you cast an eye over it,' Fullalove offered, generously. 'When it's finished.'

'It's not finished?'

'Barely begun.'

'Well, that's something,' Plant said.

'So I thought we might go along to Writers' Week.'

'Why?'

'Get some ideas.'

'On how to write? You've got to be joking.'

'I know how to write.'

'So why?'

'I thought we might go and check something out.'

'Something?'

'Someone.'

Plant nodded wisely. In due course Fullalove would tell him. If that was what Fullalove wanted. If it wasn't, he wouldn't. Plant had no intention of giving him the satisfaction of being asked. And then being implicated in whatever seedy enterprise eventuated and told, 'Well, you did ask, didn't you?' No, he wouldn't ask.

'Rock Richmond,' Fullalove said.

'Rock Richmond?' Plant said. 'Is he talking there?'

'A session devoted to his genius. In profile. Face to Face. Mouth to Mouth. Didn't he tell you?'

'No, he didn't,' Plant said.

'That's interesting,' Fullalove said.

'Yes,' Plant agreed.

'Holding out on you.'

'Maybe. Though when you think about it, probably not. Why should he have told me? Unless it was relevant to the theft.'

'Depends what he's going to be talking about,' Fullalove said.

'I guess it does,' Plant agreed.

'Incidentally,' Fullalove said, 'when he was robbed of his computer and his back-up, did he happen to have a second back-up somewhere?'

'He did, as a matter of fact,' Plant said.

'So why would he have hired you if he still had his second back-up? And don't say to stop the material turning up in the media. We know that's nonsense.'

'I don't know,' Plant said. 'Maybe to give the impression that he didn't have a second back-up.'

'That's what I was thinking,' Fullalove said.

Chapter 11

The phone cut into the tranquil morning with its burden of grief. Plant answered it apprehensively. It was Maggie Richmond.

'Rock's dead,' she said.

'Dead?' Plant said. He remembered to express sorrow before asking how.

'Can you get over here?'

'Sure,' Plant said.

'Right away?'

'Right away.'

'So what happened?'

'The police aren't saying. But they found his car up at the lighthouse and he was in it. Dead.'

'Dead,' Plant said.

'Dead,' Maggie Richmond said.

She was in black again, whether for mourning this time or still for work Plant could not tell.

'So natural causes or foul play?'

But if it had been natural causes she wouldn't have called him, would she?

'What do you think?'

'Heart attack?' Plant offered.

'He was perfectly healthy.'

'You can't always tell.'

'I could,' she said.

'So how?'

'He was shot.'

'Shot? With a gun?'

'That's how you usually get shot,' she said.

'Was it...?' He faltered, but there was no polite periphrasis. 'Suicide?' he asked.

'The police aren't saying.'

'But they're on the case.'

She gave a contemptuous laugh.

'You could say that,' she said. 'For what it's worth.'

Doubts about the police were not unfamiliar to Plant. He did not subscribe to the condescending contempt of the liberal élites for their Inspector Plod caricature. He was more inclined to the corruption and conspiracy view espoused by Fullalove: that the police were in it up to their ears through the informers they ran, reselling the drugs they seized, stealing BMWs to order, organizing armed robberies, all the usual stuff. He waited to see which way Maggie Richmond would go.

'You don't sound confident,' he said.

'I wouldn't have called you if I had been, would I?' she said.

'I suppose not.'

'You don't have to pussyfoot with me,' she said.

She was adroit, there was no denying. She made sure he had to spell it out himself.

'You think they're incompetent? Or bent?'

'I didn't say that,' she said, coming down heavy there.

'No, you didn't,' Plant agreed. He smiled, as if to defuse the tensions: or ginger them up.

'I'm sure you know the score,' she said, smiling back.

Plant shrugged modestly.

'Police are police,' he said.

'Yes, well, I've gone up against them a few times for my clients.'

'Just a few times?'

'Most times,' she said. 'Every time.'

'Who won?'

'I won.'

He didn't doubt it.

'So,' he said, 'they don't love you.'

'No, they don't.'

'Ah,' Plant said.

'Am I so unlovable?' she asked. She looked across at him, as dewy eyed and seductive as a recently widowed, successful female person barrister could look. Or needed to.

'Not at all,' Plant said. He surprised himself at the enthusiasm with which he said it. It seemed to surprise Mrs Richmond, too. She blushed. Or blenched. Changed colour, anyway, a couple of times between pink and white.

'So,' she said, 'I need someone to do some legwork.'

The menial stuff, Plant reflected. Like hiring a gardener. Maybe he should add 'Lawn Mowing' to his card.

'You think your husband's death was connected with his book?' he asked.

'No idea.'

'But you're hiring me.'

'Got to hire someone.'

'Your husband hired me about the stolen computer.'

'You ever find it?'

'No.'

'Well, you won't need to bother now.'

'The two things might be connected.'

'So in that case keep looking,' she said.

'Was he depressed?' Plant asked.

'Oh, for heaven's sake, you met him.'

He had met him, true, but it didn't answer the question.

'It's hard to tell,' he said.

'No it isn't,' she said. 'He was never depressed. He floated along the surface of life without a care in the world.'

'Sometimes that can be misleading.'

'Not with Rock. What you saw was what you got. A bit less, generally.'

'What about his career?'

'What career?'

'His writing.'

'Career!' she said. 'It was just a hobby. Kept him out of mischief. I brought in the money. He just amused himself.'

'He was due to speak at the Byron Writers' Festival.'

'So?'

'Could he have been worried about that?'

'Worried? Rock?'

'Could he have felt unable to face an audience?'

'Nonsense. He loved being in front of an audience.'

'And he wasn't afraid there might not be an audience. That he was out of fashion, or something.'

'He might have been out of fashion but that never stopped him. There'd have been an audience. Rock always made sure of that. He'd have phoned round letting people know. He'd be on the phone for hours. And he'd have told the festival organisers who to email.'

'You said his writing was just a hobby. You don't think he took it more seriously than that.'

'No one else did.'

It may have been true. Harsh but true. But perhaps Rock had had deep, unexpressed ambitions. Plant left them unexpressed.

'Maybe it didn't keep him out of mischief,' Plant suggested. 'Maybe it got him into mischief.'

'What on earth do you mean?'

'The book he was writing.'

'What book?'

'The one that was stolen. The history of the alternative. Maybe he'd stumbled across something. That's maybe why it was stolen and why he was killed. If he was killed.'

'You've got to be joking,' she said.

'Maybe somebody told him something.'

'Who would ever have told him anything?'

'Somebody he interviewed for the book.'

'What would be the point? You think he'd have listened? He never listened to anyone. He was incapable of listening. He just burbled on non-stop. He was like a permanent creek that never dries up.'

'Until now,' Plant said.

'Yes. Well. Look, he was a kindly enough affectionate person in his self-centred way. As long as it didn't put him out he'd be amiable. But he wasn't your crack reporter. Forget that. Basically all he was interested in was himself. And indulging it.'

'So why would someone kill him?'

'I can't think that anyone would. Except from boredom.'

'Boredom?'

'He was basically so boring someone might have decided to kill him before he bored them to death.'

'Is that how you felt?'

'Me? No, I was used to him. I didn't take a lot of notice, to be honest. I just let him chatter away.'

'Was it a happy marriage?'

'Happy?' she asked. 'I never really thought about it. We pretty much lived our own lives. It's a big house. I didn't kill him, if that's what you're thinking.'

'No, I wasn't thinking that,' Plant said. Not that he mightn't.

'But you don't think it was suicide?' he continued.

'Why would it be?'

Plant shrugged.

'You think he found marriage to me so terrible?'

Plant went for the impassive number.

'You're playing the impassive number,' she said. 'Yes, naturally, you think he'd kill himself to get away from a bitch like me. But he wouldn't. I can assure you. If there'd been any chance of it he'd have done it years ago. No, we got along. He needed me. He needed the income to live on in the style to which he'd become accustomed. All that nonsense about alternative lifestyles, that was just fancy dress, the only lifestyle Rock ever wanted was the high life. So you can forget that.'

'I don't have to forget it,' Plant said. 'I didn't think it to begin with.'

'Well, aren't you a nicely brought up young man.'

'I try,' Plant said.

'You certainly do. Nobody could accuse you of a want of trying.'

Plant smiled. An unfriendly observer might have called it a simper.

'You're a self-satisfied little fucker, aren't you?' said Mrs Richmond.

'I don't know about that,' Plant said.

'I do,' said Mrs Richmond.

Plant figured it was best not to argue.

'So,' he said, 'what exactly do you want me to do?'

'Nose around,' she said. 'See what you can turn up. I've got other sources, obviously.'

'Other sources?'

'You don't work in a legal office without access to information.'

'I suppose not.'

'You suppose right. But you have your sources too, presumably. Hopefully.'

'Oh, yes,' Plant said.

'Good. I can't take time off to look into it. I'm flat out. But I don't trust the police to do a thorough job.'

'Naturally.'

'So,' she said, bringing the audience to an end.

'One last thing,' Plant said.

'Go on.'

'You don't think he might have written something about one of those drugs cases you defended?'

'Which one?'

'I've no idea. You told me you'd defended a lot of dope cases.'

'I don't recall that. One of your sources, was it, Plant? You've been checking up on me already?'

'You said you'd run up against the local police.'

'Possibly that's how you interpreted it,' she said. 'I may have said I felt I might not get the fullest cooperation from the police. In terms of keeping me informed, that is. I am confident they will investigate to the best of their ability. But as for my cases, I never talk about them. Not in the remotest way.'

'Not even to Rock?'

'Especially not to Rock.'

'Why especially not?'

'We kept our professional lives to ourselves. Not that Rock could ever be called especially professional. I didn't want to hear about his writing, he didn't want to hear about my cases.'

'Never?'

'Never.'

'Even though some of your cases might have involved people or situations he was writing about.'

'Which ones?'

'Might have, I said.'

'Rock wasn't one to dig deep. He liked to take things as they come. If they didn't come, he didn't go running after them. He wasn't an investigative reporter. Basically, he was just lazy. That's why you can forget any idea of suicide. It would have been too hard. Too much trouble.'

Perhaps she wasn't as heartless as she seemed. Perhaps it was her way of concealing grief. If so, she certainly did a good job. No doubt she mistrusted the police. A lot of people did. But Plant was not sure that she trusted him either. If she didn't believe Rock's history of the alternative was of any significance, why had she hired him, when he had failed to turn up any trace of it? Maybe that was why. Maybe she felt confident he would turn up nothing about Rock's death either. But to hire him would demonstrate concern, make it look like she wanted to find the killer, if there was a killer. Or perhaps it was a way of monitoring the investigation. If she was on less than friendly terms with the local police, they would tell her nothing. But if she had her own investigator on the case, that might be a way of seeing what turned up. It might be a way of ensuring that nothing turned up, too, while all the time looking concerned. The fact that she had hired him did not mean that she hadn't killed Rock herself. Or arranged for Rock to be killed. Using the theft of the computer as part of the disinformation, making it look like Rock was being targeted for something. She could have stolen the computer herself, for that matter, to make it look like that way, all part of a sustained plan. The face that she so patently put no value on Rock's writing may not have been mere wifely contempt. Or the contempt for her one-time media star but now fading husband may have been true. But she still didn't have to value his work to steal it. It may all have been a careful smokescreen, using the theft as part of the plan; or opportunistically using the fact of the theft as the moment to bump him off, making it look like the events were connected. All those years in the dock defending villains would have shown her how successfully to sow confusion. And she was an innate, intuitive confusion sower. Plant, confused as he now was, had no doubt about that. But as to whether he had been hired to find something out or not to find something out, he had no idea. It would be hard to be more confused than that.

Except for mentioning it to Max, and more recently to Fullalove, Plant had not made any inquiries about the missing computer. He had phoned the media as Rock Richmond had requested, given him the list of who he'd contacted and gone back and phoned a few more people Rock had thought of, vain imaginings as they were, and that, Rock Richmond had made clear, was it. He did not want Plant making any more waves. In no way had he wanted an active investigation. 'If you happen to hear anything, let me know. I'll pay. But don't go looking.' And that had been it. No retainer. End of case. He wondered if he was expected to do more for Mrs Richmond. It was hard to tell.

Chapter 12

Fullalove was sympathetic. Either that or laboriously sardonic. Or maybe simply stoned and genial and finding everything amusing.

'Hey, but that's bad, man, losing a client. That's really tough. Bad for business.'

'Bad for business?'

'Doesn't look good, losing someone. You're supposed to protect them.'

'I'm not a bodyguard.'

'Clearly not.'

'I wasn't even hired any more.'

'You weren't on a retainer?'

'No.'

'So how come you were still working on it?'

'I wasn't.'

'Why not?'

'He didn't want anyone making waves.'

'You can see why,' Fullalove said.

'Why?'

'Got himself killed, didn't he.'

'I don't know that there's any connection.'

'You've got to be joking. People don't just get robbed and then killed without a connection.'

'Maybe,' Plant said. 'His wife doesn't think there's a connection.'

'Well, that's a start,' Fullalove said. 'Puts her in the frame. Reckon she did it?'

'She's just hired me to find out who did. If anyone did.'

'Old trick,' Fullalove said, 'you know that.'

'Yes,' Plant said, 'I do know that.'

'There she is, successful career lady, supporting this superannuated bum. Probably not even superannuated, probably never even paid into a pension fund. So he's just a drain on resources. And out of date. Not even last year's model. He gets himself mysteriously robbed. Perfect opportunity to get rid of him. Make it look like the two are connected. She might even have done the burglary in the first place. She's got access. Means, motive and opportunity, what else do you need?'

'It had passed my mind,' Plant said.

'But you don't buy it?'

'The jury's out.'

'Yeah, well, the longer it's out, the longer she pays you I guess.'

'That's true,' Plant agreed. It was one positive note in an otherwise unpromising business.

'So is it suicide or did someone do it for him?'

'I don't know. The police haven't said yet.'

'I suppose it wasn't natural causes?'

'Parked in his car? Probably not.'

'Where did they find him?' Fullalove asked.

'In his car up at the Cape Byron lighthouse.'

'What did he drive?'

'What did he drive? What's that got to do with it?'

'I don't know till you tell me.'

'A Porsche Carrera. Silver metallic finish.'

'Well, it could have something to do with it. Not the colour. But the size. You reckon that's a convenient car to kill yourself in? A bit constricted for messing around with guns, I'd have said. Wouldn't it have been easier just do it at home? I mean, it wasn't like he was gassing himself or taking pills or slashing his arteries. Just a quick gunshot to the head.'

'I don't know that it was to the head.'

'Wherever.'

'I take your point,' Plant said. He didn't see Rock asking to borrow his wife's BMW. But he could just have walked out onto the gravel driveway. Or shot himself in his den. Perhaps he hadn't wanted to mess up the house and grounds. Well trained by his wife.

'What sort of gun?'

'I don't know. She didn't say.'

'Was there a gun there?'

'I don't know. Why?'

'Why? Come on, Plant, wakey-wakey. It could make a difference between suicide and murder. If there was no gun, it looks like someone else did it.'

'But if there is one, it's suicide?'

'Not necessarily.'

'Of course not. How naive of me.' Plant tried the heavy sarcasm but Fullalove disregarded it. It was something he had learned to disregard over the years.

'So what's your take on it?'

'The way I see it,' Plant said, 'is Rock Richmond was making one last bid for fame and glory. Make or break. He saw it as his last chance to get his name back in lights. He was still hung up on making it, still looking for that bestseller in the sky. He figured this was it.'

'I can relate to that,' Fullalove said.

'He'd got all the reports he'd written for whoever he'd written them for. He'd got forty-something years of history.

Maybe there was something in the reports, something he'd been reporting on. Maybe there was something sensational. Or maybe he found out something doing his interviews. World-shattering stuff he said it was.'

'And it got him robbed and then it got him killed,' Fullalove said.

'Yes.'

'Why not?'

Plant put another log on the fire. The flames rose up and licked around it. Outside, the chorus of frogs rose and fell. The moon silvered the gums and camphor laurels.

Fullalove rolled himself another smoke from Plant's diminishing stash. Plant poured himself a rough red from the Riverina.

'So what's the story?' Fullalove asked. 'What did Rock Richmond know?'

'Why would he be writing reports for the government?'

'Do you know that he did? Did you see any?'

'No. He wouldn't show me. Said it was confidential.'

'Did you buy that?' Fullalove asked.

'Not especially.'

'Maybe he was bullshitting. Maybe there was nothing there.'

'Maybe,' Plant said. 'I did consider that. But I think it was for real.'

'If there was some secret government stuff going on he'd have had to have signed some Official Secrets Act.'

'It's possible.'

'But you say he was writing a book.'

'Maybe he didn't care,' Plant said. 'Maybe he was dying. Maybe he wanted to get it written while he could and didn't care about breaking the Act. What reprisals could they do? Maybe he was going to publish it posthumously.'

'Could be.'

'But my bet is he wanted one last bid for fame. His last great grab at wealth, sex, drugs. No worry about AIDS or addiction when you're past a certain age, what does it matter, you're not going to live much longer anyway, you'll be dead before the virus incubates, and what does it matter about having a habit, as long as you can afford it, so there's no need to worry about anything. This was his last chance to make it big and reap the rewards.'

'It certainly was,' Fullalove said. 'He's not going to have another one.'

'And he underestimated the risks. Someone knew what he was doing and decided to stop him.'

'Something stopped him, that's for sure,' Fullalove said.

'And just before he was due to speak at the Writers' Festival. Where he might have talked about it. Though I doubt it.'

'True. But somebody might have thought he might talk about it. Decided they couldn't take the risk that he might.'

'So if it was secret government stuff, maybe the secret services knocked him off.'

'Always a possibility,' Fullalove agreed, 'in our democratic society.'

'Which might explain why he wouldn't report it to security when he was burgled.'

'Why would he?'

'If he'd incorporated material from the government reports into what he'd written.'

'You know for sure he didn't report it?'

'I don't know anything for sure. But that's what he said. He said he'd told the local police but if security got into the act it would frighten off the people he was interviewing. But maybe he didn't want security knowing he'd incorporated classified material into the stuff on his computer. Which he maybe shouldn't have been holding anyway. Maybe he was afraid that if they found out it had been stolen there'd be ...'

'Reprisals,' Fullalove said. 'I think that's the word you're looking for. Steal, burn, rob, kill. Search and destroy. That sort of stuff. And it looks like there might have been.'

'It does,' agreed Plant.

'Unless it was drugs,' Fullalove said, rolling himself another joint. 'There's always drugs.'

'There won't be if you keep on smoking at this rate.'

'Then we'll buy some more. No problem. It's a market economy.' Fullalove passed the joint across. 'Here, relax. There'd have to be a lot of drug stories in a history like that. Could be somebody didn't want him telling them.'

'Like his wife.'

'Or something his wife told him.'

'Possible,' Plant said. 'Except she claimed she never told him anything.'

'Possible.'

'Except she might have.'

'Possible, too.'

They subsided into passivity, watching the patterns in the fire.

Chapter 13

Plant took off for the beach for his morning health walk and shell-gathering. Fullalove generally woke late. Plant decided it was safe enough to leave him alone in the house if he was sleeping.

He greeted the fishermen and the dog-walkers and the horse-riders and the bicyclist. He set off heading into the wind so it would be behind him on the walk back. A couple of pelicans cruised past. Beyond the surf the gannets plunged headlong into the sea.

Afterwards he stopped at the phone box by the general store and phoned Max.

'Plant here,' he said, 'I thought I might drop by later, you be in?'

'I'll be in,' Max said.

Some calls you didn't make from your own phone.

It wasn't only that he was running out of dope. Fullalove's arrival had cut a swathe through his stash. Once it got down to a certain level Plant started to get anxious for the future. But it wasn't only that. It was the possibility that Rock Richmond had known something that had got him killed. What was needed was some further confirmation, or at least a lead, that might turn the possible into probable, something that might offer a lead on Rock Richmond's death.

'I'll come with you,' Fullalove said.

Dealers didn't like you bringing along observers when you were doing a deal. On the other hand it would be good if Fullalove bought his own dope instead of consuming Plant's. And on the third hand, Plant was not eager to leave Fullalove home alone in his waking hours. He feared both fire and phone bills. All in all, it seemed best to take him along. Especially since he was intent on coming.

'Speed on Tweed,' Fullalove read out. 'What's that?'

'Not what you think it is.'

'It is, man. It's a sign. Drugs.'

'It's a car race.'

'No, it's a sign about drugs. That's what this case is about. Drugs.'

'You believing in signs, now?'

'I've always believed in signs,' Fullalove said. 'It's just that living in the city you don't tell people. But up here it's cool.'

'Is that so?'

'I reckon. Look, Weed Heads,' he read triumphantly from a defaced signpost. 'See, the man said to look for a sign. And there it is.'

It was a worrying sign in itself, Fullalove habituating himself to alternative life, taking to it, settling in, seeing signs. Next thing he'd be suggesting they eat a Hunza roll. It was not something Plant felt happy about. Not at all. He had no objection to the Hunza roll if it meant a long and healthy life. But having Fullalove settling in, that was not something he looked forward to with any equanimity.

When they got to Nimbin Fullalove insisted on stopping. Plant usually drove straight through. It was not a place he especially wanted to be seen loitering in. He preferred to score his dope less publicly. Apart from the vibe factor. The possessed, the lost, the panhandlers and the predators. Astral parasites, free-floating entities, enveloping ectoplasm hung along the street, tossed here and there in the breeze like tumbleweed. But Fullalove was adamant.

'Get the feel of the place,' he said.

'I know the feel of it.'

'You may,' Fullalove said. 'I haven't been here for years.'

They sat in the car.

'Hey man, how about that?' Fullalove said, surveying the psychedelic rainbow colours of the shop fronts. The psychedelia maybe a bit faded, like old sarongs, washed by the rains and bleached out by the sun. But it was there.

Nimbin Hemp Embassy, declared the sign. Hemp Bar, declared another.

'Seems cool to me,' Fullalove said. 'Though it probably isn't. I guess we'll see.'

'Do we have to?' Plant asked.

'We can't stay sitting here in the car,' Fullalove said.

'You think they'll think we're cops?' Plant asked.

'Not in a bottom-of-the-line Hyundai,' Fullalove said, getting out.

'It's a time warp,' Fullalove said, ensconced in a chair outside a café and surveying the passing parade. 'Amazing. It's like it was forty years ago. All these young kids dressed like hippies. Where do they come from? They can't be the original ones unless they found the elixir of youth. Are they their kids? They're all so young and yet they still look the same.'

'Probably grandchildren,' Plant said. 'Or runaways.'

Hippy-looking grandparents hobbled past, wasted, wizened, but still in their coats of many colours, their caftans, their motley. Their hair was grey and thin but still as long as it had ever been, their eyes as blank and glazed as in the best of times. Backpacking tourists disgorged from a minibus. Plant shuddered.

'Where's your sense of adventure?' Fullalove asked.

'Adventure?'

'Nostalgia, then.'

'Nostalgia?'

'Nostalgia must be pretty adventurous for an old fellow like you.'

'I don't think of myself as old,' Plant said, sniffily.

'Bet these kids think you are,' Fullalove said.

One of them came up to them.

'You want hydroponic or organic? Regular or skunk?' he asked Fullalove.

Fullalove grinned in happy surprise, the space where his missing teeth had been glistening with saliva and delight.

'Hydroponic?' he queried. 'Why would I want hydroponic? I can see the point in the city but why out here? In nature,' he added, gesturing to all the nature around.

'Helicopters, mate, gotta hide it from the choppers.'

'Go for organic,' Plant advised.

'Why's that?'

'You never know what they've fed the hydroponic on.'

'It might be interesting.'

'It isn't,' Plant said.

'How about skunk?'

'Too heavy. Messes with your brain.'

'Sounds appealing,' Fullalove said.

'Tell you what,' Plant said, in inspired desperation, 'why don't I just leave you here to soak up the atmosphere and work out what you want and I'll pick you up on the way back?'

'Cool,' Fullalove said.

The dealer waited for Fullalove to decide on his order, earring glistening in the morning sun. Plant left them smiling their missing teeth smiles at each other.

Chapter 14

'My condolences,' Max said.

'Condolences?'

'On losing your client.'

'Ah, yes.'

'So the case is closed.'

'Yes and no,' Plant said.

'So you here for dope or in the course of your inquiries?'

'A bit of both.'

'The widow footing the bill now, is she?'

Plant said nothing.

'I take silence for assent,' Max said.

'Can't stop you.'

'Not an honest fellow like you. She must be loaded, she'll be able to afford you. Not that you'd be expensive, would you? Just pricey enough to cover your dope habit.'

'You don't come cheap, Max.'

'Try Mrs Richmond then. Some of these growers she gets off pay their account in kind with a car-boot of grass. You might get her to do the same for you. Sort of thing lawyers like. No paper trail.'

'Is that so?'

'So they say.'

'Tell me more about the military connection,' Plant said.

'Are we getting into conspiracy mode?'

Plant shrugged.

'Roll yourself another,' Max said. 'Should do the trick. Keep the paranoia percolating.'

The refreshing thing about Max was that no question was too recondite, no suggestion was too over the top or off the wall. If Plant had asked about the presence of aliens from outer-space in the counter-culture, Max would have provided him with the known sightings. Like the UFO that landed at Corndale decades ago. He had preserved the happy openness of the alternative, something that the urban intelligentsia and their literary-academic cabals had long since lost.

'So tell me.'

'What did you have in mind?'

'You said a lot of the alternative settlements had military connections. Military personnel.'

'Sure, there were a few ex-army types moved up here. There was a war going on.'

'So what's new?'

'True. But what was new then was conscription. It involved a lot more people. In the end there were fifty thousand Australian troops went to Vietnam. Most of them got a taste for dope there and when they came back, except for the five hundred and four that didn't, some of them decided to stay stoned and drifted up here. So statistically you'd expect a fair few military types and a fair few draft dodgers.'

'So was there a sort of military ambience?'

'Not really. It was all make love not war. Though army surplus clothes were chic as well as cheap, so there were lots of alternative types who dressed in battledress tunics and camouflage gear. Proclaiming solidarity with Castro and Che Guevara and General Giap and Chairman Mao. Though in the case of the devotees of Mao it tended to be designer silk shirts which were a bit pricey for hippies on the dole. More Rock Richmond's style.'

'Uh-huh,' Plant said.

'So you could say it was just part of the culture of the times.'

'What was?'

'The military note.'

'Uh-huh,' Plant said again.

'You don't sound convinced.'

'I just find it interesting that there were military types around in a so-called counter-culture.'

'You're in the country, mate. The country is military. That's the way it is. It's where the army camps are. It's where the soldiers come from and where they go back to. Like the police. They're all country kids. You've seen all those RSL clubs with their old field guns parked out the front. They've always been big on the military in the country.'

'I thought the alternative were against all that.'

'Sure, some were. But there were some that weren't. There were people who'd done their time in the army and came out and became hippies. The point is, whether they were for the military or against it, the military was there anyway. A familiar presence. A landmark. Nothing you'd think to remark on. One of the guys organizing the Aquarius Festival had been in the army. For years the mayor of Byron was an ex-SAS man. Another one ran one of the communes. It's just the way it is.'

'Maybe.'

'You want a drugs for arms conspiracy?'

'I hadn't thought of it.'

'I don't believe you. But even if you hadn't you will now. You shouldn't mess with that stuff.'

'What stuff?'

'Conspiracy theory. It's bad for your head.'

'But fun, though.'

Max laughed. He rolled up another one.

'And where would we be without fun?'

'Corporate executives. Making a lot of money.'

'There was sure a lot of money made up here,' Max said. 'There were enough dope rackets without bringing in the arms trade. No shortage of rackets, no shortage of work. Planting, irrigating, harvesting, driving, selling, investing, laundering. A whole infrastructure.'

'Must have involved a lot of people.'

'It was the local economy,' Max said.

'Was it all independent growers, or were they subsidiaries of some parent company?'

'Ah,' Max said, 'some things you never do find out. Some things it's best not to inquire about. It's not impossible it was run like a franchise operation.'

'Where did the seeds come from in the first place to grow on a commercial scale?'

'Good question,' Max said.

'And the answer?'

'I never did hear an answer,' Max said.

He drew on the joint reflectively.

'Mind you,' he said, 'the CIA was around.'

'Really?'

'Some CIA connected types were involved in coastal development. CIA, ex-CIA, Nugan Hand Bank, Pat Boone.'

'What's Pat Boone got to do with it?'

'He was one of the investors in the Ocean Shores development.'

'Along with the CIA?'

'Apparently.'

'Why would that be?'

'No one ever explained. A good investment opportunity, maybe. Certainly the Nugan Hand Bank was supposed to be mixed up in drugs for arms overseas. So why not here? But it doesn't have to have been anything operational. Just some species of greed. Or a way of making money to finance some operations they didn't want to have to go to Congress to try and get approval for.'

'Maybe Rock Richmond turned up something in his history.'

'I doubt it.'

'Why?'

'What would he turn up?'

'Who knows?'

'Anyway, he'd be more likely to keep things quiet.'

'You reckon?'

'He was more your traditional patriot type. A nice enough fellow, but not your natural rebel.'

'That's what Fullalove said.'

'Fullalove? Is he still around?'

'"fraid so.'

'I'd be afraid of him, too.'

'Why's that?'

'Who's he working for?'

'No idea.'

'That's what I mean.'

Plant nodded.

'So, was he on the payroll?'

'Fullalove?' Max shrugged. Some things best left unsaid.

'I meant Rock.'

'Ah, if we knew everyone who was on the payroll.'

'So maybe Rock was on the payroll to play down the military connections.'

'There was nothing to play down. It was all public. People had been in the army because they'd been drafted. They wore jungle greens because they were cheap.'

'Maybe being public was a way of concealing something,' Plant suggested.

'Good dope, isn't it?' Max said. 'Keeps the conspiracies rolling. You want to buy a deal or you just want to keep on smoking mine?'

'I'd like to do both,' Plant said.

'Fair enough.'

'Tell me about the SAS man?'

'Which one? There's a few around.'

'You said one ran one of the communes.'

'Well, in a manner of speaking. Communes were supposed to sort of run themselves. Communally, you know. But he was the force behind it.'

'Is he still there?'

'Jake Illingworth? Not any more. He's still around but the commune isn't.'

'What happened?'

'The way of the world. Privatisation. They slogged it out for a while but then it broke up into individual ownership. Multiple occupancy. All the collective stuff went.'

'And that's why he went?'

'He stayed there for a while.'

'Was it a political issue?'

'Was what?'

'The privatisation.'

'Just greed. They all set out with idealistic notions of community but after a few years of screwing each others' partners and sharing joints, they regressed to their primal state.'

'Which was?'

'The origin of the family. Private ownership. Defined boundaries.'

'And was this ideological regression fraught with political debate?'

'Not that I recall,' Max said. 'It was the mood of the times. Economic rationalism. Seemed to suit everybody.'

'Including their erstwhile SAS leader.'

'Why not? He'd prospected a nice spot for his own place.'

'But he left.'

'Yes.'

'Was he forced out?'

'Not according to him. Says he'd reached retirement age.'

'How old was he?'

'Mid-forties.'

'The age they retire from the army.'

Max laughed. 'You're determined to see a plot. You think he was army all the time?'

'Could be. It would explain his leaving in his forties. That's when they usually retire. Go out on a pension. Not a huge one but enough to get by with. Especially if you get some other sort of job like running a security firm or a caravan park. What's he doing now?'

'Running a caravan park.'

'You're joking.'

'There are no jokes.'

Plant shook his head in wonderment.

'Anything else I can tell you?' Max asked.

Chapter 15

Plant picked up Fullalove at the café. He was sitting there with an unusual look of contentment, nodding at the spontaneous street theatre of freaks and tourists. Most of them gave him a wide birth.

'You look like a criminal invader from the dark metropolis,' Plant said.

'Sure, man.'

'Or an undercover cop.'

'Same difference.'

'I'm surprised anybody would do business with you.'

'He was probably an undercover cop trying to establish street cred.'

They got in the car and drove off and Fullalove produced his stash from inside his shirt.

'Took your advice,' he said. 'Top grade organic. Fat free, wheat free, gluten free, no added sugar, no preservatives.'

'We didn't really need it,' Plant said, ungraciously. 'I could have got you a deal.'

'Where's your sense of adventure?'

'I moved up here for the quiet life.'

'Never hurts to diversify the source, anyway,' Fullalove said. 'Gives you something to compare. Stops you losing the buzz from getting habituated to the one strain. Divide and conquer.'

He rolled up a sample as they drove along. The Nimbin rocks shimmered behind them, magical and mysterious. Fullalove lit up and took a breath and choked. The car filled with fumes and sputum. Plant took the joint from Fullalove's shaking hand and sucked on it. The trees leaned over.

A car coming the opposite way flashed its lights, then a second one, and a third.

'Must be police,' Plant said. He dropped down below the speed limit. Not too far below so as to be conspicuous, but far enough.

'Get rid of that joint. Quick.'

Fullalove didn't argue. For all his propensity to present an opposite view on principle, automatically to generate a counter-version, in this instance he was admirably forceful and steel-willed. He nipped out the burning joint between finger and thumb, and swallowed it. Then he emptied the contents of the ashtray through the window, roaches, ash, and the small change Plant kept to feed into parking meters and to buy produce at roadside stalls. Dollar and two dollar coins alongside five and ten and twenty-cent pieces.

'That's probably ten or twenty dollars you just threw out,' Plant said.

'Worth it at the price,' Fullalove said, wiping a tissue round the inside of the ashtray and throwing it through the window. Now littering could be added to the charges.

A few more cars flashed their lights before they saw the police car on a grass verge, the driver beside the road with a speed camera.

'It's just not worth it, smoking in the car,' Plant said. 'Cops see you passing it across, or even just smoking, they can see you're inhaling, they'll pull you over.'

'Maybe not worth it for you. You'd get the saliva test, seeing as you were driving. They don't test passengers, though.'

'I'd say I was the victim of passive smoking. So they'd test you all right.'

'We could both say we were victims of passive smoking,' Fullalove said. 'They wouldn't be able to convict both of us, and they'd never be able to work out who was actually smoking, so we'd probably get away with it. We'd be fine.'

When they came to the sign to the Clarrie Hall dam Plant took the turn off the road. They drove up and parked and looked at the serene water and rolled a couple of smokes.

'Far out,' Fullalove said, resting his eyes on the stretching water. His expression was developing a new serenity. Fascinating the way a love of dope could develop into a love of nature in the right environment. He was back on the road to ancient hippydom.

'Remember the Hunzas who lived to a hundred and something on Hunza pie?' Fullalove asked. 'Why don't we go down to Billinudgel and get a Hunza roll at The Humble Pie. Keep the dream alive.'

'Which dream was that?'

'The seventies. The alternative. Nostalgia for a better life. Remember the Hunzas.'

'Could do.'

'You know how to cook Hunza pie?'

'No idea.'

'Exactly. So if you don't know how to cook it, we got to go where we can buy one. Besides, it's part of the legend.'

'Which is, the Humble Pie or the Hunzas?'

'Both man. They both came out of that culture. Like *Alice's Restaurant* and *Another Roadside Attraction* and *Vineland*. Part of the ambience, man. The world of Rock Richmond.'

He didn't even sound sardonic. He was mellowing.

'So let's do it. It's a chance to get the feel of the environment, sample the local cuisine. Eco-tourism they call it now. And it's healthy, man. Low fat wholemeal pastry.'

'How do you know?'

It didn't sound like a typical item from Fullalove's usually highly politicised information store. In regard to food Fullalove was basically omnivorous and undiscriminating. Or was he changing?

'Heard it on local radio.'

'When do you ever listen to local radio, you're always watching TV?'

'When I'm out in the ute. In the middle of the night when I can't sleep. All sorts of occasions. Amazing what you hear. Good to diversify your information sources.'

It was good dope. The sort that induced a gentle nostalgia for rainbow psychedelics and Hunza pie. Just as long as Fullalove didn't start asking for magic mushrooms.

They looked at the water for a while longer.

'Apple pie would be good, too,' Fullalove said. 'A culinary trip down memory lane. The traditional way of life. Something sweet.'

'As American as apple pie,' Plant said.

'Americans don't have a monopoly on apple pie.'

'I thought you thought they had a world monopoly on everything.'

'Shit man, you're sharp today. No wonder you sailed through that police ambush.'

'If we stay here too long they'll think we're terrorists planning to poison the water-supply,' Plant said, the mention of police triggering in a bit of classic dope paranoia, the still calm surface of the reservoir the mirror of his mind, the hidden depths full of things.

'Could be interesting,' Fullalove suggested. 'See who they send along.'

'I don't think so,' Plant said. 'I think we should just go. Now.'

They went. Mount Warning bowed its peak in polite farewell.

Plant lit a fire. His Norseman slow-combustion burner was one of the joys of his life. The simple joys of the man of the land. When the evenings were cold enough, and they could be cold enough in Spring or Autumn, not only in Winter, then a fire was a source of deep satisfaction. Especially when he could get the wood-man to deliver wood, which was never easy. But he had wood and he had twigs and he had fir cones. And there was enough newspaper from Fullalove's compulsive purchases to start the fire, so everything ignited the way it should.

After the first blaze had settled down he put a couple of potatoes and a couple of sweet potatoes into the ashes. Fullalove looked on in unfeigned puzzlement, but said nothing. He was immersed in conspiracy theory and when he raised his eyes from his book, they invited no conversation. Which suited Plant. After an hour he wrapped a couple of heads of corn, still in their leaves, in aluminium foil and put them in the fire too. It was his solution when he felt unwilling to mount a major cooking operation or to go out for take-away. Let the natural forces cook for you. He had always seen the appeal of minimalism in effort as in art.

After another half hour he took everything out. The

potatoes were blackened and charred, the sweet potatoes had begun to split open, the corn steamed as he removed the foil and the sheath of leaves. He sliced the potatoes in half, opened up the sweet potatoes, served them up with the peeled corn.

'Aren't they burnt?' Fullalove asked suspiciously.

'Just eat the insides.'

'Are you sure this is safe?'

'Absolutely.'

'I won't get carbon poisoning?'

'Just eat the inside of the potatoes.'

'Is that it?'

'You can grate some cheese on it you want. Feel free.'

'Where is it?'

'Cheese is in the fridge. Salt and pepper are on the table.'

Fullalove probed into the potato cautiously. He took a tentative jab at the sweet potato. The deep orange flesh was soft and tender. He gnawed some nuggets of corn off the cob.

'Amazing,' he said.

'You like it?'

He reflected. 'Not bad,' he conceded. 'Not bad at all. And no additives. No oil, no cooking fat, they just cook on their own.'

'Well, someone has to put them in the fire,' Plant said. 'And take them out.'

'Fair enough.'

'And light the fire,' Plant added, for good measure.

Fullalove dug into the potato and chewed on it.

'It actually tastes like potato. I'd forgotten what potatoes tasted like.'

'The secret,' Plant said, 'is to make sure they're cooked.

Don't take them out too soon. They can't hurt staying in there, they only get a bit more charred on the outside.'

'Can you eat the skins?'

'Why not?'

'Did you wash them?'

'The fire would've killed off any bacteria. But yes, I did wash them.'

Fullalove crunched into the least blackened piece of potato skin.

'Amazing,' he said. 'You don't need oil, you don't need cooking fat, you don't need electricity. Just light a fire. So why do people bother with ovens?'

Chapter 16

In the middle of the night Fullalove opened Plant's bedroom door and called out.

'Hey, man, are you awake?'

'I am now,' Plant said.

'I've got it. Survivalism.'

'What?'

'That's what it's about.'

'Tell me in the morning.'

'I already told you. That's it. Survivalism.'

Plant slept with the word worming around his dreams.

'I was lying there thinking about that dinner. The way it cooked itself. No electricity. No gas. Just in the fire. No pots, no pans, no implements, no equipment. And then I ashed my joint in one of those shells you collected. And then it came to me. The sponges. The fir cones. Survivalism.'

'So you said,' Plant said.

'That's what it's about.'

'What is?'

'The whole movement. The communes. The settlements. The hippies. Survivalism.'

'Surviving what?'

'Nuclear war. That's what they were all afraid of. Our rulers. All through those years. What would happen if there was nuclear war? What would happen if all the cities got totalled? What would happen if there was no electricity, no oil, no gas, no resources? What would they do? Well, what they'd do is what you've been doing, go out into the country and collect firewood and fir cones and cook in the ashes, and scoop things up with shells.'

'Really?'

'Didn't you know that?'

'No,' Plant said.

'It's pretty obvious. I mean, what else would it all have been about? Some spontaneous upsurge of love and peace? They may have thought that, the hippies. But they were just the laboratory rats for the scenario for the next war and its aftermath. The big one.'

'And that's it?'

'No man, it's a lot bigger than that. But that's the basics. Cooking in the ashes. The phoenix rises from the post-nuclear wasteland. All these communes, all these hippy settlements, they were part of an experiment to see if people could survive. See if they could go back to the land and start from scratch. Build some huts. Start families to begin repopulating. Develop social organisation. What the ruling class were afraid of was a return to barbarism after the place had been nuked. So they set up these controlled experiments. See if people could get it together. See how they'd survive.'

'See what they'd do for ashtrays?' Plant said.

'Exactly.'

'Survivalism,' Plant said, 'is that a word?'

'It is now,' Fullalove said. 'Risen from the ashes.'

'And who set all this up?'

'The government. The military. The secret services. They had to do studies to see what would happen.'

'Why?'

'Why? To write reports, that's why. To pass around

committees, that's why. It's a bankrupt ruling class, you know that. But they've got to pretend they know what's happening. They've got to give each other the illusion they're in control. Otherwise the share market crashes. So they set up projects to predict the future. Plan what happens when the resources run out, when the polar ice caps melt, when the sea level rises, when the tsunami hits, when the bomb goes off. You name it, they've got a project to give the answers. The answers don't mean anything, of course. But it creates the illusion someone's thinking about the problems and so with that taken care of they can go on making money and having wars and destroying the environment. Business as usual. And if anyone asks they can say, oh, we did a study on that, yeah, we got a report on that.'

'So it's all an illusion.'

'Life is an illusion,' Fullalove said, 'you know that.'

He beamed his emaciated Buddha smile. Fullalove the enlightened.

'Yes, I know that,' Plant said.

'The point is that something was going on. It wasn't just a spontaneous move to the hills. It was a government project. Or series of projects. Run by the government or the military or someone. Doesn't matter who. The point was it was being run. Now, did your friend Rock Richmond know this? Is that what he was writing about and is that why they stole his computer and bumped him off? Was he part of the project from the beginning? Was he sent up here as the observer to write regular progress reports? Or is he an innocent, did he just stumble on something when he was writing his book?'

Fullalove was in full flow. He held up his hand when he

needed to take a breath, to prevent Plant from interrupting, and then plunged back in.

'Now, next question. Was it just this? Survivalism? Or was something else going on? Usually when they set up something, they can't resist running some other project alongside it. Saves on set-up costs. So we have to ask, was there a deeper level secret project?'

'No idea,' Plant said.

'Pass us the dope and let's think about it, what would it be?'

'Dope growing, Max reckoned. Or maybe dope was the bait to get people up here.'

'Maybe,' Fullalove said. 'Dope's pretty basic to all these schemes. They have to be self-financing so they don't get scrutinised. It's always better not to ask for funds. Generate your own. And dope's the easiest way.'

'Drugs for arms,' Plant said.

Fullalove looked at him.

'I think you've got it,' he said. 'Got it in one. You're a genius, mate. Sometimes.'

'Thank you.'

'Drugs for arms,' Fullalove intoned.

'So where are the arms?'

'That's what we have to find out.'

'Oh, no,' Plant said, 'no we don't.'

'Where's your sense of adventure?' Fullalove asked. 'Where's your intellectual curiosity? Where's the spirit of inquiry?'

'Leave it alone,' Plant said.

'Arms caches,' Fullalove said. 'That's what it is. Either Rock Richmond found out about them or somebody thought he'd found out. Somebody heard him banging on about some scoop and they were afraid that was what he'd discovered. So they lifted his files, and when he wouldn't take the warning, they got rid of him.'

'How does this connect with survivalism?'

'Have you read any of the survivalist stuff?'

'No.'

'You just sort of collected sponges and shells and cooked in the fire spontaneously?'

'How else?'

'Where did you get the idea from?'

'I don't know. I used to collect shells as a kid I imagine. We used to cook potatoes in the ashes of a bonfire. You'd have a bonfire in the garden and when it had burned down you'd put the potatoes in the hot ashes and take them out a couple of hours later.'

'I'm not asking for the details.'

'I thought you were.'

'So you don't buy *Survivalist* magazine?'

'No, I've never heard of it.'

'Can you get it up here?'

'I've no idea.'

'It might give us a clue.'

'About what?'

'Somewhere along the line, if not from the beginning, all this surviving off the land stuff got mixed in with gun freaks. The right to bear arms. Militias.'

'Militias?'

'They mightn't call themselves militiamen. They'd take some sort of cover. Rifle clubs. Gun clubs. Skirmish games. Lots of weird stuff goes on, people camouflaging themselves and blackening their faces and running around the bush at night with rifles.'

'And these wouldn't just be overgrown schoolboys having fun.'

'Doesn't mean it's not serious.'

'I knew you'd say that.'

'You better believe it.'

'I'll do my best.'

'Stay-behind units. They had them all over Europe after the Second World War. There was a big outfit in northern Italy. Others in southern France. They set up arms caches in the hills. I reckon that's what they've been doing here.'

'Stay behind units?'

'Supposed to be for when the Soviets or the Chinese invaded, but you can treat that with a grain of salt.'

'Can I?'

'Yes.'

'Why?'

'Even the most crazed neo-con patriot wasn't going to be taking on tanks with a rifle or a machine gun.'

'Is that what they cached?'

'Pretty much.'

'So what were they for?'

'To put down the locals. Put down looters if the bomb went off. Street fighting in case a communist government got itself democratically elected. Which would have happened in Italy, getting elected, if the USA hadn't poured millions into making sure it didn't. Buying votes. Buying parties. Buying media.'

'Do you have any evidence that they've been doing it here?'

'Buying votes, buying parties, buying media? Of course they have. Just look at the papers, look at the politicians.'

'No, I mean evidence of militias, arms caches.'

'Evidence?' Fullalove said. 'What do you mean, evidence?'

'Like proof.'

'You want a notice or something? ARMS DUMP – KEEP OFF! POST-NUCLEAR SURVIVAL PROJECT – KEEP OUT!'

'No, obviously not.'

'Well, that's something.'

'But there must be records. Or speculations. Hasn't anybody written about it?'

'Ah, the papers again,' Fullalove said. 'Our sterling independent free press. If it was written about in them, then it would have to be true.'

'Has anything been published?'

'Who knows? And what would you find out if it had? You think something as sensitive as this is going to get written up? The truth all spelled out?'

'But it's been written about in Italy and France, you said.'

'Mixed in with a ton of disinformation.'

'It was all a long time ago, why would they care now?'

'And things have changed?'

'The Cold War's over.'

'Is it?'

'Isn't it?'

'You really think so?'

'Isn't Communism finished?'

'Don't you believe it, comrade.'

'No?'

'The haves will always be organizing against the have-nots.'

'And that's what it's about?'

'What else has it ever been about?'

'Tell me.'

'Communists, Nationalists, Islamic fundamentalists, they're just the flags under which to organise. The struggle never ends. And the ruling class is never going to give up. You think they're going to let someone reveal their strategies?'

'Even if they're obsolete.'

'Survival projects, arms caches. How can they ever be obsolete? They'll always be there. Different techniques, different technologies, different weapons. Bows and arrows, crossbows, machine-guns, nuclear bombs, chemical and biological agents. The point about them is always the same. To kill people. The caches might have different contents, but the purpose is still the same. They're not going to be telling people where they're hiding them or what underground command centres they've built or what back-up communication networks they've put in place.'

'I suppose not.'

'You suppose right.'

'So there's no point doing an internet search.'

'Don't be crazy. They'd be onto you right away. That's what the internet's for. Go to a jihadist website and there's a swat team waiting on your doorstep before you sign out. Why do you think there are all those conspiracy websites listing the names of secret service operatives and giving the addresses of drone-controllers? They're to lure you in and then ...'

'And then what? I can't see them having a whole lot of political trials,' Plant objected.

'Who said anything about trials?'

'So if you can't look it up on the web and anything in print is disinformation, how do you know these arms caches exist?'

'Disinformation is always about something. You don't need to believe the details. But enough came out to make it clear there were arms caches all over Italy and France. You can bet it's no different here.'

'In case the Indonesians invade?' Plant suggested. Sceptically.

But Fullalove had no time for mere derision.

'Indonesia, forget it. For internal insurgency. I keep telling you, the enemy's within as far as the ruling class is concerned. They're not protecting us against foreigners. They're protecting themselves against the electorate.'

'The electorate?'

'Their own people, mate. That's the enemy they have in their sights. Dissidents. Subversives. Communists. Unionists. Ratbags like you.'

'Me? What about you?'

'You and me. They go on about enemies abroad so they can have armies and intelligence agencies to put down the enemy at home. That means us. The people.'

The fire blazed, the flames curling round the logs. They could as easily curl around human limbs. Bishop Latimer, Giordano Bruno, the anonymous witches. More light, more light.

Chapter 17

Outside in the night the parliament of frogs croaked through its proceedings, gusting waves of dissent and debate. The owls cried menacingly around the valley as they flew their secret missions.

'It still wouldn't hurt to have some evidence,' Plant said.

'They've always had decentralised caches to supply all the reservists and para-military: army reserve, territorial army, national guard, school cadet corps, university regiment, ROTC, civil defence, state emergency services. Some you know about in a semi-public sort of way, some you don't. Secret militias are only an extension of what they've always done. They're just the undercover version of the official story. The parallel society. The state within the state. But they're not going to go public about it, are they? That would take away the whole point.'

'Which is what?'

'Secrecy. They might have some things they're open about. Boy Scouts...'

'Boy Scouts?'

'Why not? Boy Scouts. Girl Guides. Hitler Youth League. Police-Citizens clubs. Rifle clubs.'

'I don't believe it.'

'Suit yourself. Anyway, that's just what they admit to. Sort of. Admit they exist, even if their real purpose is never admitted. But they're going to have to have a secret network, too, aren't they? One that never gets mentioned. The crucial one. To round up the dissidents with when the crisis hits.'

'Are they?'

'I would if I was them,' Fullalove said. 'It's not as if they don't need it. And it keeps the arms manufacturers busy. Makes money. Keeps up the employment figure.'

'So where are these arms caches?'

'Out in the bush. What do you think starts the bushfires? Australia. California. Southern France. Greece. Portugal. Arms caches hidden away in the sticks and blowing up. Old ammunition getting unstable. Why do you think the National Parks and Wildlife are such a paramilitary organisation? You've seen their army uniforms. And their fleets of off-road four-wheel drives. Military jeeps, identification code letters on the bonnet in case they need to call in aerial back-up. Why do you think the inquiries into bushfires never come up with anything? Forestry service, national parks, they never get indicted. Why not? Because it's all part of the apparatus of the secret state.'

'I can believe it,' Plant said.

'Yes, it's neat,' Fullalove reflected. 'You've got all this stuff going on up here, people growing dope, people chanting Hare Krishna, people eating magic mushrooms, people with recording studios, people with guru complexes setting up settlements. It would be easy enough to set up a few experimental projects run by the government. Maybe there were a number of them set up on different models. The variety of settlements provided good camouflage. No one was going to remark on another one. Just more crazies and hippies.'

'So Rock Richmond was commissioned to report on the government ones or on all of them?'

'He'd have to report on all of them. The ones they didn't

set up they'd use as controls. You need controls when you run an experiment.'

'And he knew what was going on?'

'Depends on how much they told him. Maybe there was tight need-to-know security in place and they just gave him a general brief. Or maybe they just gave him a general brief but he was required to report on some specific groups and they'd leave it up to his judgment which others he covered. That's why they'd have hired someone like him: his judgments were the same as theirs. Good establishment lad. So he just monitored how things developed. When they gave up scavenging for shells and started making pottery. How they maintained internal discipline: or failed to. Whether they survived best with rules or without them. Probably monitored the folk musicians and rock 'n' rollers and bush poets too. Keeping a check on subversive verse and dodgy lyrics.'

'So were they setting up survival experiments, or setting up reserve militias?'

'Could've been either, but it was probably both. If they've got the military sponsoring survival projects, you can bet they'll mix in some other military project. And they had lots. That LSD research of Timothy Leary's was funded by the U. S. Navy. Maybe they had a magic mushroom project going here. Conditioning and deconditioning. And if they'd got people practising surviving up here, here's where you need militias and arms caches. To arm them or put them down, depending on how things turned out. They could've decided to run one of the communes on militia lines. An armed cult. Like Waco. Or the Oklahoma bombing. That sort of thing. Or they could've set up a militia taking recruits from different settlements, so the militia and the caches aren't tied in to any specific commune, but are run separately. Gives them the chance to have their people in lots of different communes. Or they could figure on drawing extra troops from the different settlements when the time came. Could be either.'

'Or both,' Plant said.

'Sure, or both. There could be a militia commune and there could be another militia formed from people from a lot of different settlements. Try the options. See which looks like mobilizing or surviving the best.'

'Max didn't seem to find the military stuff significant.'

'Well, he wouldn't, would he?'

'Why wouldn't he?'

'Well, it's his beat, isn't it?'

'What's that mean?'

'He's on the payroll.'

'Is he?'

'Of course he is.'

'Why do you say that?'

'He must've been busted some time, have to have been, the amount he deals. And then they'd lean on him. He's paid to keep his ear to the ground. Or given immunity to deal a bit. He's not going to be telling you everything he hears, I wouldn't think. He'd just say what he's told to say on that. Even though he might see you as a fellow law-enforcement type. Shared values and all that. Except he's obviously checked up on your file and knows you're not reliable. Not sound, Plant.'

'How do you know what my file says?' Plant asked. 'You been checking up on it too?'

'I don't need to look at your file to know you're unsound,' Fullalove said. 'Drug dependency, alcohol abuse, indiscriminate heterosexuality, negative attitude to authority, soft on subversives, dubious library borrowings, incomplete voting record.'

'Maybe,' Plant said. 'Maybe, not. It still doesn't answer the question.'

'Doesn't it?' Fullalove asked.

Plant put a couple more logs on the fire. It blazed up cheerfully. There was a certain cosiness about it all, the adequate supply of dope from Max and Nimbin, the halva from the Mullumbimby supermarket, the rough Riverina red from the bottle shop, and the old, familiar, inevitable aura of paranoia.

'You want to check out some of these communes tomorrow?' Plant suggested.

'No.'

'No?'

'No way.'

'Why not?'

'They give me the creeps, man. I've never enjoyed going to those places. Always some weird vibe. I'm all for free love and free dope. Nobody could be more into them than me.'

He smiled his stoned, lecherous smile. Plant felt himself involuntarily shuddering.

'But it's like there's no such thing as a free smoke. I always felt there was some horrible price I was going to have to pay. The people running the show always seemed seriously weird. Not just bossy and heavy. All that peace and love stuff and those rainbow-coloured clothes. But you could feel the steely purpose beneath. They were up to something. I used to think it was sex. Some weird sex thing they had in mind for later down the track. When the fire died down. But maybe it wasn't that. Maybe it was guns.'

'And you don't want to check them out? See what they're up to.'

'It's all over, man. We're into terminal globalisation now. Forget self-sufficient communities. Forget independence.'

'If you say so.'

He was relieved, he realised. He had no wish to go back into the past. He'd never felt he'd belonged there, any more than he belonged in the present. But the present was inescapable, up to a point, dope apart, whereas a self-inflicted journey to the past had nothing to recommend it. A reverie, perhaps. A dope-assisted recollection, maybe. But going there, doing it. No. He agreed with Fullalove. It had been, it had happened, it hadn't reformed the world. The world now, as far as he could see, was a worse place. Afghanistan. Iraq. Libya. Syria. Australia, for that matter. But there were things about the past he preferred not to confront: hopes, failures, heavy dudes and dudesses. All called dudes now. Gender was finally leaving the language, completing the process of shedding begun in the nouns and adjectives and definite and indefinite articles a millennium ago. Why go back? The irrelevant revolution had happened and now was now.

But he gave it one more try. He was conscientious. Whatever else he was, Plant told himself, he tried to be thorough.

'So where exactly would these arms dumps be?'

'Who knows? National parks. Areas of extraordinary scenic beauty. Heritage sites. Multiple-occupancy communes. Fundamentalist churches. Private schools.'

'Should we look?'

'Are you crazy?' Fullalove said.

'You don't feel we need to know.'

'We know,' Fullalove said.

'But we don't know where.'

'We don't need to know where. It's enough that we know.'

'Saves tramping around the bush,' Plant agreed.

'The point about investigation,' Fullalove said, 'is that it's a cerebral activity.'

'If you say so.'

'Leave well alone,' Fullalove said. 'This is the age of virtual reality. Let's keep it that way. Purely conceptual. We know they're there. We don't want to find them and get shot to pieces.'

'Let alone covered in leeches and ticks.'

'Never.'

'So none of the old John Buchan stuff. Mountain scree and highland burns and crofters' cottages and deer hunters taking pot shots at you as you hide in the heather.'

'No way,' Fullalove said. 'You can forget that.'

'Fair enough,' Plant said.

Chapter 18

'You going to the funeral?' Fullalove asked.

'It's a memorial service,' Plant said. 'They haven't released the body yet.'

'Whatever,' Fullalove said.

'I suppose I should. I did know him.'

'Briefly,' Fullalove said.

'I think I will.'

'Charge the hours to the merry widow. Say we were proceeding with our enquiries.'

'We?'

'I'll come along and keep you company. See if anyone looks suspicious.'

'I was going to pay my respects.'

'Well, as long as she pays your hourly rate, why not? I'll keep my eyes open while you're being respectful.'

Rock Richmond's wife may not have thought much of Rock's writing, but she gave him a celebrity send-off. Perhaps he had specified it in his will. The church was filled with once beautiful people in their faded finery, flowing black chiffon scarves, spreading natural fibre hats with black ribbon. A few journalists in grubby black suits and some lawyers in smart black suits filled the back rows. Odours of patchouli oil and Indonesian clove cigarettes mingled with the heady emanations of marijuana. The vicar beamed down upon them all.

There were a few obligatory prayers. Then the vicar

who had been, if not a rock star, at least some sort of pop singer, sang a song he and Rock had written together. The vicar had written the music and Rock the words. The congregation joined in with the choir for the chorus.

'All together now,' said the vicar.

He picked out the key for them on his electric guitar.

All together it was.

The recording engineer gave a thumbs-up from the choir stalls.

'I think we've got a hit on our hands,' said the vicar.

The congregation clapped and whistled.

'A truly religious experience,' said the choirmaster, standing in front of the altar, clapping his hands and inclining towards the vicar. 'Divine words. Heavenly music.'

The vicar beamed like God the father in *Paradise Lost*.

'Praise the Lord!' called out one of the congregation.

'And pass the ammunition,' responded another, in an army slouch hat.

Then a Klezmer band played a Jewish jig and an Irish band played an Irish jig. A toothless flautist played a toothless flute solo. The man in the army hat came forward with a bugle and played the Last Post. A line of a dozen sixty-something year old surfies made a covered way of long boards for the congregation, in lieu of the coffin, to pass beneath.

'See what I see,' Fullalove said, from a vantage point in the churchyard.

'The tragic mourner?'

'Yup. The weeping hippy.'

'Is she hippy or artistic?'

'Certainly theatrical,' Fullalove said.

'Not unattractive.'

'But painful.'

'Our Lady of Pain, you reckon.'

'The sort of thing you'd've reckoned he'd go for?'

'Maybe.'

'Would you?'

'Maybe.'

'But it would be a bad idea.'

'I guess so.'

'It could be his daughter.'

'I don't think so.'

'How about the clergyman's daughter?'

'Could be the clergyman's girlfriend,' Plant said.

'Maybe she's one of those wailing mourners you can hire.'

'It's certainly an impressive display of grief.'

'Or guilt,' Fullalove said.

'You reckon?'

'Always a possibility.'

'I think you're being cynical,' Plant said.

'Never hurts,' Fullalove said.

They caught up with her walking down the street. All veils and voile and red-nosed snuffles.

'Do you want a lift to the wake?' Plant asked.

She turned to look. Plant half expected her to take to her heels and run. But she didn't. She gave a well brought up gracious smile, the way they taught them in private girls' schools.

'Thank you,' she said. 'That's very kind of you. But no.'

'You're sure?'

'I don't think I'd be welcome,' she said. 'In fact I know I wouldn't.'

'Why's that?' Fullalove asked.

'Oh ...' she said, gesturing with her hand, as if that explained everything.

She dug around for a tissue and blew her nose.

'Excuse me,' she said.

'Why's that?' Fullalove repeated.

She shook her head.

'I'm not family,' she said. 'Not as far as they're concerned, anyway.'

'Nor are we.'

'I was a friend of Rock's,' she said.

'So?'

'So,' she said.

'That sort of friend,' Fullalove said.

Tears welled up in her eyes. Plant could feel panic approaching. Weeping women made him as uneasy as strong women. Often the weeping women turned out to be very strong.

'Would you like a coffee or something?' he offered.

She hesitated, calculated.

'Maybe a herbal tea,' she said.

Plant looked round uncertainly. 'Let's see if we can find somewhere,' he said. Cafés were not the sort of places he hung out at much these days.

'The whole street's full of cafés,' Fullalove said.

They sat there uneasily on the uncomfortable chairs on the sloping forecourt or pavement or compromise between the two, smoking prohibited, not a hope of getting away with blowing a joint any more, unlicensed. She sipped at her herbal tea. Plant sipped at his. Fullalove blew across his cappuccino to cool it and sprayed them with foam. People in beach clothes and swimwear and holiday casual and Hawaiian retro sat at the tables around them. Plant felt very conscious of the blackness they radiated. Drug-dealers from the big smoke come up to score drugs. Even worse, terrorists. They looked like something out of a bad movie. It wouldn't take much for someone to respond to the government's terror campaign. Help protect Australia from Terrorism. Small pieces of information from members of the public can help keep Australia safe from terrorism. Police and security agencies are working hard but you could help them complete the picture. If you see anything suspicious call the 24-hour National Security Hotline on 1800 123 400. Our trained operators take every call seriously and you can remain anonymous. Remember, every piece of information helps.

Even if you think it's probably nothing, the smallest piece of information can be valuable. Calls to the National Security Hotline have already contributed to investigations. If something doesn't add up, speak up by calling the National Security Hotline.

'Rock was my teacher,' she said.

'I didn't know he taught.'

'Oh yes,' she said.

'What did he teach?' Fullalove asked.

'Creative writing.'

'Ah,' Fullalove said. 'That.'

'He was an inspiration.'

They let it hang there a moment, something to rise up to, where the smoke would have been, an ectoplasm of desire and aspiration.

'Where did he teach?' Fullalove asked.

'TAFE,' she said. 'Technical and Further Education.'

Fullalove shook his head silently.

'How long had he been doing that?'

'I don't know. I'd only just started.'

'But he was a friend.'

'He was my lover,' she said.

'Ah,' Fullalove said.

She sniffed and dug out another tissue.

'He didn't need the money, did he?'

'Everyone needs money,' she said, in her thin little voice.

'His wife's loaded.'

'She may be. But he needed his independence.'

'Ah,' Fullalove said.

'And he loved to teach. He believed in sharing his gifts.'

'Generous fellow,' Fullalove said.

'He was,' she said. 'And now he's dead.'

She wept some more.

Plant tried to catch Fullalove's eye, rein him in, call him off, but Fullalove knew that and kept his gaze fixed on the girl.

'So were you friends of his?' she asked.

'Yes,' Plant said.

'No,' Fullalove said.

'Which is it?'

'I knew him,' Plant said. 'He didn't.'

'And how did you know him?'

'I was doing some work for him.'

'What sort of work?'

'Private.'

'Confidential?'

Plant nodded.

'Give her your card,' Fullalove said.

'Do you have a card?' she asked.

He handed it to her. She read it.

'What about your friend?'

'He doesn't have one.'

'Is he an investigator too?'

'Fullalove, tell us,' Plant said. 'Are you an investigator too?'

'Journalist,' Fullalove said.

'Oh, like Rock.'

'Not like Rock,' Fullalove said.

'Plant,' she said, putting the card away into her capacious Moroccan soft-leather bag. 'And Fullalove,' she added, as if committing the names to memory.

'And your name is?' Plant asked.

'Madimi Dee.'

'That's an unusual name,' Plant said.

'My parents are unusual people.'

'What sort of name is it?' Fullalove asked, ethnic categoriser, recorder of social class.

'Madimi?' she said. 'A spirit name.'

'A spirit name,' Fullalove said. 'Well, I'll be damned.'

'There's forgiveness for everyone,' she said, 'if you truly repent.'

Then she cried some more.

Chapter 19

They arrived at the wake late. It was not quite as bad as being late for a funeral, but Maggie Richmond's 'Good of you to make it' was not without a certain tart quality.

'Help yourself to a drink,' she said, making it clear she wasn't going to be serving them.

Fullalove sniffed at the patchouli- and marijuana-laden air and said he'd rather have a joint.

'I don't think we've met,' Maggie said.

'He's a journalist friend of mine,' Plant began.

'Don't bother with the name, then,' Maggie said. 'I shan't remember it.'

'Maybe I should've asked for a line of coke,' Fullalove said as she walked off.

Plant walked off too. In the end he settled for a white wine.

Uncle Toby greeted him from a strategic position beside one of the tables, a plate in one hand, a sausage roll in the other, the Order of Australia lapel pin proudly pinned into the lapel of his grey linen jacket. Like an elderly vicar or a college chaplain, one of the dodgier ones with an earlier career in the military or continuing connections with the secret state.

'Dear boy, we haven't met for ages. Where have you been?'

'I haven't been anywhere,' Plant said. 'How about you?'

It was the right answer.

'Kazakhstan,' Uncle Toby said with a self-satisfied

smile.

'Business?' Plant asked.

'Now what sort of business would I have in Kazakhstan?'

For a retired professor of whatever he had professed to profess, it was hard to think of more than one or two businesses that might have taken him there. Or that had taken him anywhere else, for that matter, over the years. But before Plant could offer any suggestions, Uncle Toby assured him 'Pure pleasure.'

'What sort of pleasure?' Plant asked.

'Romantic yearnings,' Uncle Toby said. 'I always wanted to go there. Ever since I read of "a rose red city half as old as time."'

'When did you read that?'

'Longer ago than I care to admit.'

'And what did you do there?'

'In Kazakhstan?'

'Yes.'

'Travelled, dear boy. Travelled around. Sampled the local cuisine.'

He wiped his lips with a paper napkin and helped himself to some more smoked salmon.

'Was it good?'

'Good? The cuisine? No, I wouldn't say that it was good.'

'You should write travel articles.'

'You think so?'

'You've been everywhere.'

'I have, haven't I? And you think I should make a point of telling the world all about it?'

'You're telling me.'

'Ah, but that's different, dear boy. You are but you. A

singular you. But the national press is something else. I never had poor Richmond's eagerness to pour myself into print. Best to keep out of the newspapers in my observation.'

'You prefer the *éminence grise* approach.'

Uncle Toby smoothed down his silver sheen.

'Exercising power and influence and telling people about it are not compatible activities. The pressure to publish or perish has not produced unqualifiedly positive results.'

'You advise putting nothing on paper.'

'The careful scholar's motto,' Uncle Toby agreed.

Professor Toby Oates had always been a very careful scholar. It was not true to say that he came from an era when scholars were gentlemen and not expected to publish. It was an impression he had tried to cultivate, but he was not that old. Old enough to be retired, though you didn't have to be very old for that any more. But not as old as to date from the era of the gentlemen scholars on whom he would seem to have modelled himself. Gentlemen scholars with a line into power. There was something ominous about his presence at Rock Richmond's wake. Plant had not expected to see him there. Rock and Uncle Toby was not a connection Plant had ever made. But there was a certain inevitability about it. A classic economy, elegant in its way.

What Uncle Toby was actually into, Plant had never known. Uncle Toby cultivated a bland geniality that suggested he was into nothing much except fussing around and enjoying the good things of life like free food and wine and travelling the world and floating in and out of conferences and seminars, and not writing. But it was a blandness that nonetheless could not resist implying that there was more to this than met the eye. Its unpersuasive innocence was redolent of the world of the secret state. And it was not just the influence of Fullalove that made Plant think that.

'You knew Rock Richmond, then.'

'Alas, poor Richmond, I did indeed know him well,' Uncle Toby said. 'One of my boys.'

'He was a student of yours?'

'A graduate student.'

'That must have been years ago.'

Uncle Toby gave his old Tiresias look before continuing to make serious inroads into the food in a way that put Fullalove to shame.

'I suspect it was,' he said.

Plant reflected. Uncle Toby's boys were young men he had nursed through their MAs and PhDs and steered into the worlds of government and diplomacy and academia and journalism. So had Rock done a doctorate? It was something Plant had not known. It certainly wasn't listed in any of the on-line biographical entries. There had been no framed degree hanging on the wall of the den.

'So did Rock do a doctorate?'

'Not exactly,' Uncle Toby said.

Of course not. Nothing could ever be exactly so with Uncle T.

'He came up to Brisbane on a postgraduate scholarship. It gave him the chance to live in his blessed Byron Bay and surf, and still fulfil the requirements.'

'What requirements were they?'

'Oh, residence, attendance at classes. Those things used to be taken seriously. Before the day of the degree by correspondence. Or virtual education on the internet. He said Byron was only a couple of hours away so he could attend graduate seminars. It was more like three hours in those days, of course. But nobody really knew that. Nobody in any position to make difficulties.'

'But you knew.'

'Well, I'd never set out with a stopwatch and timed it.'

'So he commuted to Brisbane.'

'Hardly commuted. But he came up once in a while. He kept his appointments for supervision. Not that he needed much supervision, of course. The good ones never do.'

'And he was good?'

'He was fluent. He had no problem putting things down on paper.'

'Good things?'

'Good enough.'

'And he lived down at Byron and surfed and smoked and generally had a good time.'

'I imagine so. His topic was youth culture. So he was well-situated for research in the field.'

'And then what happened?'

'Did anything happen?'

'You said he didn't exactly do his doctorate. Did he drop out?'

'Oh no,' Uncle Toby said. 'Not in any formal way.'

'But he failed.'

'Oh, no, he never failed.'

'He never completed it?'

'Well, yes and no,' Uncle Toby said, hovering over a plate of blood-red rare roast beef before snaffling up a couple of slices.

'Did he submit it?'

'I don't believe he did.'

'Why was that?'

'I'm not sure that he ever intended to,' Uncle Toby said. 'I suspect that what he wanted was the postgraduate scholarship with its living allowance.'

'While he investigated youth culture.'

'That was his topic. *Tout court*. We had much less pretentious titles for theses in those days.'

'But he never got around to writing it.'

'Oh, he was writing it. Indeed I can still recall reading chapters of it as he wrote it. Unless I read them in print afterwards, of course. Both, probably. But they certainly appeared.'

'In print.'

'Oh yes.'

'In what? Scholarly journals?'

'Oh no. Not at all. No, in the press. I imagine he got paid quite handsomely. But there again, he deserved to. He was a handsome youth in those days.'

'Really.'

'Oh, nothing further implied, dear boy,' Uncle Toby assured him, pouncing on a sausage roll and waving it in the air before wrapping his lips around it. 'He was as solidly not to say stolidly heterosexual as you are, Plant. You are, aren't you? Solidly and stolidly?'

'Solidly and stolidly,' Plant said.

'And so, I imagine, was Richmond. Though there again, not narrowly and censoriously so.'

'He didn't strike me as a narrow or censorious person,' Plant said.

'No more was he,' Uncle Toby said. 'A model of tolerance. And openness. A loss to journalism and writing. A valued chronicler of our extraordinary times.'

He reached out for some sliced ham.

'I do appreciate a traditional funeral with the traditional funeral meats,' he said. 'Try some.'

'I'm vegetarian,' Plant said.

'Of course you are, how could I forget? Then we'll just have to find you a slice of spinach quiche, and hope for your sake it's made with free-range eggs.'

'Not my sake, the hens' sake,' Plant said.

'How caring,' Uncle Toby said.

'And you gave Rock his start.'

'I? Well ...'

Uncle Toby made his braying sound. It might have been a simper, or it might have been evasion.

'Fixing him up with a scholarship so he could write about sex and drugs and rock 'n' roll.'

Uncle Toby made a bleating sound of qualification.

'Pastoral care,' he said. 'A part of one's job. A helping hand along the way.'

'You help all your students this way?'

'Horses for courses,' Uncle Toby said. 'They have different needs. Different skills. And different opportunities present themselves at different times. You do what you can to facilitate things. If you can. When you can.' He beamed. 'When you can't, you teach.'

'So you fixed him up for three years?'

'Three, was it? I think it might have been five. Some of them got extra time, if they showed signs of producing.'

'All expenses paid.'

'It was only a postgraduate scholarship. It was hardly wealth beyond the dreams of avarice.'

'But he didn't graduate.'

'No, he didn't.'

'What happened? He dropped out?'

'Oh no, he did the work. He was no slouch, the young Richmond. But once he'd written the book, he had a problem. In those far-off days a PhD had to be original material. And that was taken to mean that not only had the content to be new, but that you couldn't have published any bits of it along the way.'

'And Rock had published bits of it?'

'More than bits, more than bits. Pretty well the whole show. The articles had attracted attention. He was commissioned to write a book on youth culture on the strength of them. He received a generous advance. And he wrote it. On the strength of the book he got a job in journalism.'

'I thought he was already writing journalism, didn't you say?'

'That was just freelancing while he was a graduate student. But once his book had been published, he was signed up on staff. So he didn't need the PhD. Not the sort of thing to have in journalism in those days. They'd have laughed at you. Except in Germany. But even if he had needed it, he couldn't have got it under the regulations they had, because he'd already published the material in his book. If he had submitted the PhD first and then turned it into a book, it would have been different. But it would have been a different book, far more academic, and it wouldn't have made his name. And he preferred the idea of journalism to the university. He wanted the real world, as he called it. Don't we all? But he bizarrely identified it with journalism. For a while. Until he grew out of it. But that was what he wanted and that was what he got.'

The real world milled around them, scrabbling for food. Journalists and lawyers and beautiful people.

'But he grew out of it.'

'Yes.'

'And then what did he do? Did he try to get back into the university?'

'Oh no, I don't think that ever appealed. No, he went freelance.'

'And he made a living at that?'

'At this and that,' Uncle Toby said.

'And you kept in touch with him?'

'He wasn't so far away.'

'You saw him regularly?'

'Once in a while.'

Plant could have persisted and tried to pin down how often Uncle Toby and Rock had met. And what exactly were the this-and-that on which Rock had survived? But Uncle T would have smelled a rat. If he hadn't already. Plant certainly smelled one. And Uncle T was nothing if not a seasoned rat sniffer. Always bland and beaming and firmly on the surface. And always associated, in Plant's encounters, with the dubious and the doubtful. No doubt to Uncle T they would not be at all dubious or doubtful. Dear boys. Men of honour. My country right or wrong. Not that any of it could be pinned down. Uncle T himself seemed absolutely the typical academic. Didn't express any strong opinions, political or otherwise. Always off to a conference in somewhere exotic, or coming back from research leave at some war-torn and ravaged spot. Always keeping in touch with one dear boy or another. Always ready to have a chat and pick up a bit of gossip. Liable to pop up anywhere and everywhere.

'But don't let me monopolise you, dear boy. There must be lots of interesting people here you want to talk to.'

'Not really,' Plant said.

'No? Well, I do.' He wiped his lips and fingers with a tissue and moved away from the food table, just one last lingering look before irresolutely turning his back on it. 'Time to circulate. But why don't you give me a call? Come up and have lunch some time.'

'That would be nice,' Plant said.

'Some time soon. How about the end of the week?'

He gave Plant his phone number and turned back to check out the cold meats and replenish his plate before wandering off and seeking out some of the interesting people.

Chapter 20

Plant left Fullalove sleeping in and took his morning walk along the beach. It helped fill the day, the vast vacuities of time. It was exercise. Good for you. Life-enhancing. It cleared the head, sometimes. His head. No need to be alienated about it.

He valued its emptiness. Beach and head. Fishermen drove past in their four-wheel drives. Occasionally they raised a hand in greeting, but never stopped. Sometimes they would be standing with their rods at the edge of the surf. Sometimes someone would be walking a dog. On a crowded day there might be as many as half a dozen people if he scanned the bay as far as the eye could see in either direction. Generally, two or three were as many as he encountered. It was quite enough. Overhead a white-breasted sea eagle or an osprey would take its slow circling patrol, while a brahminy kite kept watch from a dead tree beside the dunes. The seagulls walked out of his way if he came too close.

It was best in the morning, before a breeze had blown up. Then he could sit at the edge of the dunes and relish the sun and watch the ocean for whales or porpoises. Maybe an idea would come to him about a case. Maybe not.

A helicopter throbbed along the line of the surf, emerging from the sea haze of the Tweed estuary, tracking south towards the Cape Byron lighthouse. It was unmarked, not the Sea World helicopter or the Westpac rescue helicopter or one of the television channels. It disturbed the gulls and they squawked irritatedly and flew out to sea. Plant had become used to such alien intrusions. Surveillance was a part of his world, he could scarcely complain of others in the same line of business. He disregarded it and leaned back onto the sand dune, and the quiet and the seagulls returned.

He had been sitting there a while when he noticed a figure walking down to the sea's edge, back down from where he had come. The tide was out so there was a wide stretch of sand between the dunes and the sea. He would be able to preserve a safe distance from whoever it was when he walked back, whether they were in the sea or on the beach. He had no great objection to people at a distance. As long as he did not have to encounter them. There had been a time when he had been gregarious. Now he wasn't. Fullalove was quite enough to have to encounter.

The figure was standing at the edge of the waves, delaying entering. Plant could sympathise with that. He was not one for the sudden chill of immersion. He watched idly as it hovered there, bent down and splashed the water around, before making a run and diving under the waves.

It seemed a good moment to head off, while the swimmer was out at sea. Plant took it. But as he approached closer the figure turned back to shore and emerged from the waves, like one of those Venuses more usually associated with Mediterranean waters, an antipodean Aphrodite raised among the seaweed off the shores of Byron Bay. She emerged naked, no carefully concealing shells or artistically clinging kelp, the water streaming off her, her arms waving at her side in bird-like wing motion, then rising up to sweep her hair back from her eyes, her figure slim and youthful displayed there, glistening, water beading her breasts and belly, legs long and lithe.

Plant felt apprehension. He had no objection to the female form divine. There had been occasions when he had sat on the beach and imagined moments like this. But he sensed that in recent times such fantasies had become unacceptable. Just to continue to look could get him characterised as a voyeur, a stalker, a danger to women. He could imagine himself being apprehended and arrested and incarcerated and pilloried and all the rest of it. If he continued to approach the danger would increase. If he stopped and sat where he was, his behaviour could appear even more compromising. He could try averting his eyes but would that be believed? He gave another look. Already it seemed furtive. She was standing there, neither immersing her nakedness in the waves nor running for the shelter of the dunes. He thought of pretending to look for shells. Indeed why pretend, he regularly looked for shells. But this was one of the days the tide had deposited no shells. The sands were bare, as bare and unadorned and glistening in the morning sun as the female person standing there.

He walked on. There was nothing else he could think of doing. He tried to maintain a slow but steady pace to give her time to disappear. Was that going to look suggestive, even menacing, a slow steady walk? But wouldn't a faster stride look even more threatening, assault, rape and other things worse than death? He felt like one of those ancient Greeks, about to be struck blind or turned into some rough beast for catching sight of a naked nymph. How unfair life could be to mere mortal men.

'Hi-yah!' she called out.

At least that was what it sounded like. Approximately. Unless it was a peremptory and aggressive 'Hey, you!' It didn't sound aggressive. It sounded friendly and familiar and inviting. Or was he fooling himself? It had been known.

'Come in,' she said. It still sounded peremptory.

'Come in?' he repeated. Fatuously, he realised, even as he said it.

'Have a swim,' she said.

'Oh, a swim.' Another stuttering repeat. Swim in sensual sty, the voice in his head whispered to him.

'Or a paddle,' she said.

'Dids't thou not see her paddle with the palm of his hand?' asked the voice.

She came towards him.

'Plant,' she said.

'Yes,' he admitted.

'Madimi,' she said.

'Oh, Madimi, oh, sorry,' he said, 'I didn't ...' He tailed off, conscious of sounding even more ridiculous.

'Didn't recognise me with my kit off,' she said.

'Didn't expect to see you here,' he said.

'So you did recognise me.'

'No, can't say that I did. It was out of context.'

'And what context do you see me in? Don't say you only expect to find me at funerals.'

Poor old Rock Richmond, Plant reflected. Sex and death interwove around each other like a French movie. She was slim and lithe and young and all those things. A child of nature. No ridiculous bikini marks, because she wasn't tanned. Pale white all over, wispy pubic hair apart. She hadn't spent a lot of time sunning herself on the beach, it would seem. Maybe she was starting today. Plant's lucky day.

'Or is that it?'

Plant dragged himself out of his reverie. There was no escape there.

'Is that what?'

'You identify me with funerals.'

'Not at all.'

'Well, that's something.'

He smiled nervously.

'Glorious day, isn't it?' he said.

She laughed.

'I think I'm embarrassing you,' she said. 'Let me get my sarong.'

She ran lightly up the beach towards the dunes and came back wrapping a diaphanous Balinese drape around her. She hadn't stopped to dry herself and the sarong clung tightly to her, nipples erect, belly firm, the fabric transparent as it adhered to her.

'You going somewhere?' she asked.

Nowhere fast, he reflected.

'No,' he said.

'Time for a smoke?'

'I've given up,' he said.

'Not these, you haven't,' she said.

He followed her obediently back to the dunes. She took out a ready rolled joint from her bag of tricks, and a lighter, and lit it, and inhaled, and passed it across to Plant. He took it without a murmur and sucked in the smoke of the heady herb. It was indeed just like one of those old Mediterranean tales. On the beach with Circe. The THC coursed through his bloodstream and that old familiar feeling returned. A factitious sense of well-being and the delicate bouquet of incipient paranoia. Serving suggestions: sweet cakes, sex, fruit of the forbidden tree.

Chapter 21

'So how's the investigation going?' she asked.

'What investigation is that?'

'Aren't you looking into ...?'

He let her float there, the question unfinished, unvocalised, unspecific.

She held the silence. Beneath that airy light manner and form was a steely firmness.

Plant could be steely, too. Even when he felt himself turned to jelly by the close presence of her nakedness, and going firm in inappropriate, or at least inconvenient, places.

'Aren't you investigating Rock's death?' she asked.

'What makes you think that?'

'The way you two interviewed me after the service.'

'Interviewed you?'

'It came across like an interview,' she said. 'Not a celebrity interview, either. More like a "record of interview" as the police put it. Somehow they prefer calling it that to interrogation. Or inquisition.'

'You seemed upset,' he said.

'I was upset.'

'So ...?'

'So you came and interviewed me,' she said. 'To cheer me up.'

'It wasn't meant like that.'

'No, I'm sure it wasn't,' she said. 'Why would you want to cheer me up?'

'Well, I certainly wouldn't want to make you unhappy.'

'Wouldn't you? It wasn't your intention to reduce me to tears? Isn't that nice. So you are a nice man after all. You weren't just playing the soft cop to your friend's tough one.'

She blew smoke in his face. In a printed record of interview it might have read as very simple and crass. But with the glint in her eye and the tremor on her lip, somewhere between a smirk and a sneer and a smile, to say nothing of the joint between her fingers, it came across rather differently. How exactly it came across wasn't clear to Plant. Perhaps it was up to him to make the choice. He settled for the smile and took the joint from her hands and pressed it to his lips.

'Tell me about Rock,' he said.

'I took pity on him, I suppose,' she said. 'That's basically what it was. To begin with, anyway. He was so out of touch. He tried to be hip and cool. But, really, hip and cool, I mean I don't think they'd be in the dictionary any more, would they? They're like words from a foreign language. It was embarrassing, he tried so hard. It was like he was trying to ingratiate himself with the students.'

The depressing classroom, the scuffed floor, the scratched desks, the torn, vinyl-seated chairs. And the whiteboard with scribblings never properly erased, like graffiti from some desolate, post-industrial wasteland. Even up here in this coastal paradise urban blight pursued its defacing, disfiguring path.

'They didn't actually laugh at him. They were too bored. The whole thing was a farce. It was just a way of doctoring the unemployment figures, putting people into TAFE courses so they could be taken off the dole. And it was like he didn't know that. He thought they really wanted to learn to write. Become novelists. Become journalists. As if anyone did. Or would, if they had any sense. Journalism's dead. The kids had enrolled because the course looked like a soft option. And they got this tired old man banging on about national broadsheets. He only had to look. Nobody ever had a newspaper with them. None of them read the papers. Not even the give-away tabloids, let alone the broadsheets. What broadsheets, anyway, there's only one left and none of the kids ever read it. And here he was droning on about interviewing all these people none of them had ever heard of for media they'd never heard of. And certainly never read. And as for writing short stories, forget it. None of them ever read any fiction. Why would they? They spent all their time on social media. So I guess I kind of took pity on him.'

'That was kind of you,' Plant said.

She shot him a shrewd glance, but Plant was a past master of the bland.

'Yes,' she agreed. 'I guess it was. But it was real. I wasn't being condescending or anything. I got quite to like him.'

'Quite,' Plant said.

'Quite,' she confirmed. A precise category. She sat there silent as if reflecting on it.

'And then what happened?'

'Well,' she said, 'I suppose one thing led to another. Isn't that what usually happens?'

'I don't know,' he said. 'You tell me.'

'I can't believe you don't know,' she said. 'You're just being coy.'

'Coy?' he said.

'One of those old words like hip,' she said.

'Even older, I think,' Plant said.

'Good,' she said, 'so you know what it means.'

'Yes, I know what it means.'

They sat there, back in the silence for a while.

'And then what happened?'

She drew her fingers through the sand, making tracks first one way, then the other, crossways, like the wire mesh of an internment camp.

'Well, I can tell you it wasn't a matter of being coy,' she said.

'I didn't think it would be.'

'Didn't you?'

'No.'

'You know my type, is that what you're thinking? But are too polite to say?'

'I'm not especially known for my politeness,' Plant said.

'Just for your coyness.'

He opened his mouth but nothing offered itself to be voiced.

'Got you on that one,' she said.

'Yes,' he conceded. 'You rather did.'

'I rather did? You been taking writing courses too? How to write like Henry James? Or have you been reading *The Aspern Papers* for clues on how to find missing manuscripts.'

'What missing manuscripts?'

'Rock's book that was stolen.'

'How did you know about that?'

'Rock told me.'

'He told you?'

'He told me a lot of things.'

'A lot of things.'

'I suppose I could have said he told me everything.'

'But you didn't.'

'Well, I couldn't be quite sure, could I?'

'Couldn't you?'

'No.'

'There were some things he held out on?'

'You're quite smart, aren't you?'

Was he? Plant wondered. Not that smart if she had noticed.

'You're not so bad yourself,' he said.

'Your interrogative technique.'

'You spotted it.'

'Yes.'

'Pretty smart to spot it.'

'Oh, I spotted it.'

'You're an expert in these things?'

'Not at all.'

'Past experience, then?'

'Maybe,' she said.

He laughed.

'What was he holding out on you?'

'If he was holding out, how would I know?'

'Oh, I think you'd know.'

'I can't tell,' she said, 'whether you have a very high opinion of me, or a very low one.'

Plant left that one unanswered.

'I see,' she said.

'See what?'

'Keep them guessing,' she said. 'All part of the technique.'

'If you say so.'

'Oh, I do,' she said, 'most definitely.'

Plant gave her a winning smile. Involuntarily, almost.

'I think you can take it, it's the high opinion.'

She smiled back, no less winningly.

'You do know how to treat a girl,' she said, 'don't you?'

Plant sighed.

'I don't know about that,' he said.

'Oh, I do,' she said. 'Without a doubt.'

And then the call of the Valkyries rang out from the phone inside her leather bag and she got up and fished it out and walked away to answer it, to get better reception on the flat, open beach, maybe, or to get out of earshot. And the delicate mood was shattered. For the time being.

'Gotta go,' she said, walking back.

'Duty calls?'

'Duty or pleasure.'

'Which?'

'You can't have one without the other.'

'Is that so?'

'Try me,' she said.

She winked. That young, innocent face and the knowing wink. And the all too desirable body. She gave him one last lingering look at it as she discarded the sarong and stepped into pants and jeans and t-shirt.

'You come here often?' she asked.

'Quite often,' Plant said. 'What about you?'

'I can do,' she said.

She blew him a kiss. And then she was off over the dunes and into the casuarinas and out of sight.

Chapter 22

The red light was flashing on the telephone answering machine when he got back in. He pressed play and what a drama it was.

'Plant! Are you there? Pick up the phone, will you. Plant,' it repeated, even more stridently, 'I need to talk to you.' There was a brief silence, then 'Fuck you!'

Mrs Richmond, he presumed. He called her back.

'Plant!' she shrieked, 'where've you been?'

'I was on the beach.'

'On the beach!' she yelled. 'You're supposed to be investigating a fucking murder and you've been on the beach.'

'Is it a murder, then?'

'Of course it's a murder,' she said. 'That fucking bitch killed him,' said Mrs Richmond.

'Which, er…?'

'Which fucking bitch?'

'Er, yes.'

'That fucking bitch you were running off after, you mealy-mouthed fucker,' said Mrs Richmond.

'After…?' Plant began.

'After the fucking service.'

'What makes you say that?'

'Because I saw you.'

'No, what makes you say she murdered your husband?'

'If you can't see it, there's no point telling you.'

'I don't know about that.'

'I do, you hopeless fucker,' she said.

'Should we meet?'

'Should we meet?' she said derisively. 'What sort of hopeless fucker are you, Plant?'

'Well,' he said.

'Of course we should meet. Just fucking get over here,' she said.

'Now?'

'When the fuck else do you think?'

'I'll come over now,' he said.

'Not before fucking time.'

She slammed down the phone.

'You know that cow?'

'Madimi?'

'So you know her.'

'We've met.'

'I bet you have. I saw you at the service. Couldn't wait to get your dick unzipped. Amazed you made it back to the wake. What happened, she turned you down? Or did you already have a date with the odious Oates? You play it both ways, is that it?'

He tried the 'Really!' look. The severe and reprimanding distasteful one.

'Don't pull your funny faces at me, Plant. I know what you are.'

'You do?'

'You're like my hopeless fucking husband, that's what you're like. No wonder he hired you. Ex-husband,' she added.

'In what way, Mrs Richmond?' he asked

'Don't Mrs Richmond me,' she said.

'How would you prefer I should address you, ma'am?'

She laughed. She cracked up and laughed and touched him on the arm.

'Anybody ever tell you you're impossible, Plant?'

'Yes,' he admitted. 'Frequently.'

She laughed some more.

'Well, that's something. It's not just me.'

'No, it's not just you.'

She did the pulling herself together motions. Tissues, shoulder shrugs.

'Well, that's something.'

He smiled, tentatively.

'I'm sorry,' she said.

'That's all right.'

'No, really,' she said. 'It's all been ...'

'A strain?' he offered.

'Too much.'

'I can understand that,' he said.

'You're a smarmy bugger sometimes, aren't you?' she said. She wasn't going to surrender easily.

'Just trying to be sympathetic.'

She laughed some more.

'Yes, well, tell that to the marines,' she said.

'What makes you say she killed him?'

'I know,' she said.

'How do you know?'

'I just do,' she said. 'I have this feeling.'

'Ah,' Plant said.

'Don't "ah!" me.'

'I'm sorry.'

'You better be. I've been around, Plant. I've been in fucking court year after fucking year. You get so as you know.'

'So as you know?'

'So as you know who's guilty.'

'And you think she is.'

'I know she is.'

'Do you have any evidence?'

'Evidence, schmevidence,' she said. 'Don't mess me around, Plant. Just because you fancy her.'

He said nothing. He was not into self-incrimination.

'Well?' she said.

'Well?'

'Is that true or not?'

'Is what true?'

'You fancy her.'

'I hadn't really thought about it.'

'And another thing, Plant. After all those years in court, I can tell when people are lying. You're lying.'

'Am I?'

'Yes, you fucking are.'

'What makes you think she killed your husband?'

'She was the last person to see him.'

'Do you know that?'

'Of course I know that.'

'Tell me,' he said.

'He was seeing her that night. Her name was in his diary.'

'In his diary? Why?'

'To remind himself to get it up, presumably. In case he had a senior's moment and forgot. What do you mean, why?'

'Wouldn't it have been sort of risky, writing down an assignation where anyone could read it?'

'I can assure you I wasn't in the habit of reading Rock's diary. Or anything else he wrote, for that matter.'

'You don't think maybe he wanted to be found out?'

'Spare me the theories, Plant,' she said. 'Maybe it was for his biographers. Delusions of grandeur. That's what they write about, isn't it, the sex lives of the rich and famous. Or the poor and forgotten in this case.'

'And they were meeting at the lighthouse?' he persisted.

'Apparently. You think it's making a statement? A phallic landmark for a lovers' tryst? The most easterly point in Australia. Waiting for the sun to rise, even if nothing else would.'

'Do you have the diary?'

'No, the police took it.'

'So?'

'So how do I know? The police came and questioned me.'

'Questioned you?'

'Yes, questioned me. As in helping the police with their inquiries. The fuckers think I did it.'

'Did they say that?'

'Of course they didn't say that. But they're so predictable. You can see where their questions are leading a mile off.'

'Can you?'

'I can,' she said. 'Anyway, why wouldn't they?'

'Why wouldn't they what?'

'Are you stoned, Plant? Wake yourself up and listen, will you. You're acting like you've turned into a mongoose.'

'Yes, ma'am,' he said. 'Why wouldn't they what?' he repeated.

'Why wouldn't they suspect me? They always suspect the widow. First thing in their filthy little minds.'

'So how come they told you about Madimi?'

'Madimi,' she scoffed. 'What sort of name is that?'

'A spirit name.'

'You believe that and you'd believe anything. I can tell you, Rock wasn't into spirits. Flesh was all he cared about. Eat it, grope it, poke it.'

'What did the police tell you?'

'What or why?' she said. 'What? That it was in his diary. Why? Because they were trying to freak me out. Did you know your husband was meeting someone? Of course I knew, what do they think I am, some dumb bloody hausfrau? Of course I knew he was cheating on me. He was transparent. He got that shifty look.'

'But you didn't mind?'

'I didn't have time to mind,' she said. 'I'm too busy. If it kept him from beneath my feet, so well and good. His little playmate. Saved me having to hire one for him. He always had to have his doting admirers. Made him think he was somebody. The last of the groupie grabbers. It was pathetic but it wasn't ....'

She seemed lost for a word.

'It wasn't of any significance,' she said.

Plant nodded.

'What would you know, Plant?'

'I'm willing to learn.'

She looked at him appraisingly.

'I'll think about that,' she said. 'Later.'

Plant felt things fluttering through his bodily organs. Excitement. Fear. Paranoia. The usual things.

'And he was seeing her that night?'

'According to his diary. According to the police.'

'Did he meet her?'

'I leave that to you to check out.'

'Have they questioned her?'

'I imagine so.'

'Do they suspect her?'

'No, Plant, I told you, they suspect me. They think he went to meet her and I followed him and shot him.'

'Did you?' he asked.

'No, Plant, I didn't.'

It was the same splendid view. The bay, the hang-gliders, the lighthouse. Except that the lighthouse carried another weight of meaning, now. Would she be able to stay on living there, looking out every morning with the reminder of where Rock had died? If that was where he died. Where his body was found, anyway. The site of the lovers' tryst.

'Where were you when he was killed?'

'Fuck you, Plant, I hired you to work for me, not to fucking interrogate me.'

'I'm not interrogating you.'

'Just trying to fit me up.'

'Not at all.'

'What then?'

'It just helps to know the details.'

'I was at home,' she said.

'Alone?'

'What do you think?'

Plant allowed himself a gentle sigh.

'Doing what?'

'Doing what? Doing what I'm always doing, working on my next day's court appearance. What do you think I was doing? Loading a bloody rifle and planning murder?'

'Was it a rifle?'

'I have no idea.'

'Did Rock own one?'

'Naturally. Boys' toys.'

'He didn't strike me as a shooting type.'

'Shows how wrong you can be,' she said. 'He was a fully paid up member of the Eureka Rifle Club.'

'Eureka Rifle Club!' he said.

'You sound like Archimedes when the bath overflowed. What's so exciting?'

'And where's his rifle now?'

'Where it always is. Locked away in his gun case.'

'So he didn't kill himself with it.'

'He didn't kill himself with anything, Plant. Your little friend Madonna killed him.'

'Madimi,' he said.

'Whatever. Just get moving and check her out.'

'My pleasure,' he said.

'I've no doubt. Just watch yourself. You'll find out she turns into a wizened old crone when you get her into bed.'

'You know that for sure?'

'It's always the case with evil spirits.'

'You think she's evil?'

'I certainly don't think she's any good.'

'Right,' he said.

'And I assume you plan on getting her into bed.'

'Play it as it lays,' he said.

Chapter 23

It was blazing bright sun when he left the Richmond residence. But coming down from the hills a silver cloud filled the Brunswick valley, depositing a steady drizzle over the little town of Mullumbimby. Drifting wisps of rain-sodden cloud skimmed the tops of the trees, haze covered the pastures and the golf course. Plant was always amazed at the tactility of rain. Back at his house it ran down the iron roof, trickled over the leaves in the guttering, dripped through rust holes in the guttering itself. It dripped from the leaves and the branches of the trees, hanging in globes from the grevilleas and bottlebrush, the grass bowing down beneath its weight. Everything was a fine grey gauze. It was a day to stay indoors. Fullalove sat there gazing lugubriously at the television. Plant's television. Plant's expensive subscription satellite television.

'Images of servility,' Fullalove said. 'Nothing but images of servility.'

Plant disregarded him. It made no difference.

'All these actors. Noble free spirits. Rebels. Heroes of youth. Each his own man. Or woman. Or transsexual. What a joke. What a lie. There they are, reading a script. Independence. Freedom. What independence? What freedom?'

'You tell me,' Plant said.

'They're actors. No freedom at all. Images of servility. Spouting what they're told to.'

'I imagine that's the nature of being an actor,' Plant said.

'News readers. Interviewers. The same. There they are, mouthing lies and platitudes. All scripted and screened and approved and authorised and sanitised and censored before they get anywhere near the cameras.'

'That's the way it is,' Plant agreed.

'Politicians. Just saying the party line. What the managers and spin doctors and backers have told them to say.'

'Without a doubt,' Plant agreed.

'And these are the images that rule our lives. Every day. Spewed out over the airwaves. Through the press. Every one of them a puppet. Every one of them uttering words written by someone else. Every one of them in bondage. Images of servility.'

'You don't have to watch it,' Plant said.

'I watch it to find out what they're lying about,' Fullalove said.

'How do you know that's what they're lying about? It could be deliberate distraction.'

'Of course it's distraction. That's a start, though. Whatever they're saying, you know that's not what it's about.'

'It leaves a wide field open for what they are lying about.'

'No it doesn't,' Fullalove said. 'Money and power, that's what they're lying about. Money and power, that's what it all comes down to.' He pressed the remote in irritation and switched to the fashion channel. Half-naked girls strode up and down the catwalk, breasts bared every once in a while, just to keep you watching.

'Marvellous bloody weather you've got up here.'

'Sure is,' Plant said, the rain falling steadily.

'You like this?'

'I certainly do.'

'What is there to like about it.'

'It fills up the tanks.'

'Tanks. What tanks?'

'The water tanks.'

'Water tanks? What are they? Some sort of amphibious gun ship?'

'What we collect water in.'

'Oh, man, I thought you meant like heavy weaponry.'

'Survivalism,' Plant reminded him. 'You still thinking about militias?'

'All the same thing,' Fullalove assured him. 'Water, tanks, weaponry, all a matter of survival.'

'What puzzles me,' Plant said, 'is how Richmond thought he'd get away with it. If he knew he was handling classified material, he must have known there'd be an attempt to stop him.'

'Attempt,' Fullalove scoffed. 'These guys don't just attempt. They do it.'

'Exactly,' Plant said. 'He must have known that.'

'Maybe his last bid for fame,' Fullalove said. 'I can empathise with that,' he added, reflectively. 'Get back up there. Write a best-seller.'

'Why bother?' Plant said. 'He was well off. He didn't need the money.'

'The glamour,' Fullalove said. 'The chicks. The exposure, television, talk shows, appearances, writers' festivals.'

'I can't imagine anything worse.'

'Except for the chicks, maybe. Even then ...'

Plant thought of Madimi. She'd gone for Rock Richmond

when his glamour had faded. So who needed glamour?

'If it meant getting killed, there wouldn't be any glamour.'

'Martyrdom,' Fullalove said. 'Posthumous publication. Think of the acclaim.'

'Except there wouldn't be any. It probably will never get published.'

'So he was deluded,' Fullalove said. 'Probably thought he'd get away with it. Probably thought the sort of chaps he went to school with wouldn't martyr one of their own. In which expectation he was, of course, quite correct. They'd just bump him off covertly. As they did.'

'Who, exactly?'

'SAS is the best bet,' Fullalove said, 'from what I know of them. SAS or ex-SAS.'

'And you know about them?'

'One of my areas of expertise,' Fullalove said. 'A phenomenon of our times. Breaking and entering. Trained killers. Garrotting. Unarmed combat. Or marksmen. Snipers. They train them in all this and then they let them out into the community. What are they going to do with their skills? Fascinating career changes. One minute it's all wet jobs. Next thing you know, there they are in the peace movement. Environmental activists. Running foreign aid charities. Defending civil liberties. It's always interesting where they end up. And always on hand for a spot of quiet killing when needed.'

'You think they could have done it?'

'I think so,' Fullalove said. 'Mind you, we should keep an open mind.'

Plant registered the we. Fullalove had well and truly put himself on the case.

'It could've been an accident, mind you, and they faked it up to look like a suicide. Like Hemingway. Preserving the macho image.'

'And who would've done that?'

'The wife, of course. Never forget the wife.'

'And why on earth would she have done that?'

'Image,' Fullalove said. 'But no, I agree, it's not a high probability. Much more likely she pulled the trigger herself. Or hired someone.'

'Go on.'

'She must have been pretty bored with him. Living in the past, writing about the seventies, yawn yawn yawn. While from what you say she's your up-to-date career person. Getting lots of work.'

'I imagine she met him when he was still a star, or at least an asteroid. She starts her career later and then she catches up and overtakes. While he becomes a black hole.'

'Hard to see why she hadn't traded him in years ago.'

'Too busy,' Plant said.

He thought about it. She must have been pretty fed up with Rock. Finally fed up. How had she been tolerant for so long? It had to have been an uneasy marriage. Poor old Rock, a nice enough bloke but culturally, intellectually, behaviourally out of touch, smugly satisfied with himself, chauvinistic and sexist despite all the surface trendiness. Living up here he'd been too long in the sticks, his attitudes never sufficiently challenged, surviving beyond his use-by date like some genial thick-skinned dinosaur, increasingly crass and unaware. In the city there is always some smartarse challenging you. But up in the country it was so easy to get lazy, to become the typical provincial. Not that there weren't people around who were sophisticated or lively or aware of the way the world had changed. But the people like that who came up to the country tended to do so to get away from other people. They kept to themselves. So the Rock Richmond generation could get away with living comfortably in the past. Whereas in the city there were always people who would have needled them just for the hell of it, and kept them fighting fit.

'For my money she's in the picture,' Fullalove offered.

'Could be,' Plant agreed. 'That could be why she's trying to put suspicion on Madimi. Divert it from herself.'

'She might be right. You thought of that?'

'I don't think so.'

'Our little spirit friend been working her charms on you, has she?'

'I think despite what Mrs Richmond says about not caring about her husband's carryings on, she was still jealous. So she's trying to pin it on Madimi. Her view of it is distorted by sexuality.'

'And yours isn't.'

'Well, I certainly didn't kill Rock Richmond,' Plant said. 'But as you say, his wife could have. And if she did it, she could be trying to divert suspicion.'

'I guess you'd know,' Fullalove said. 'After all, she's your client. Good to see you're looking after her interests.'

'What reason is there to think it was an SAS hit?'

'The militia angle,' Fullalove said. 'They don't want that getting public.'

'And what evidence have you got that there are any militias?'

'You just gave it to me,' Fullalove said. 'He belonged to the Eureka Rifle Club.'

'How do you know it's a militia? It could just be a rifle

club.'

'Why would Rock join it?' Fullalove asked. Rhetorically, maybe.

'To shoot things?'

'Or to monitor it.'

'You reckon there's something to monitor?'

'Could be. Be a great cover, a legitimate rifle club. But with a hidden agenda.'

'Maybe it's the sort you have to belong to in order to justify a gun licence.'

'You reckon? Only one way to find out.'

'Which is?'

'Pay a visit.'

Chapter 24

She was down there the next morning, the water beading over her all too desirable body as she lay on the sand.

'Plant!' she said, 'what a nice surprise!'

'We need to have a talk,' he said.

'Oh, must we?' she said. 'Can't we just do it?'

She fixed him with her level gaze, the clear blue eyes, the whimsical curve of the lip.

'And don't tell me you're going to say, "Do what?"'

'This is business,' he said.

'Well, it's all business to a working girl.'

'When was the last time you saw Rock?' he asked.

'Saw or spoke to him?'

'Either.'

'A couple of days before he died,' she said.

'What about the night he died?'

'What about it?'

'You didn't see him then?'

'I would have said if I had.'

'Did you?'

'Did I what?'

'Did you see him that night?'

'What is this, an interrogation?'

'Pretty much.'

'Well, aren't you the big bad wolf,' she said.

'Are you going to answer me?'

'Of course I am. Don't be so anxious.'

'Go on.'

'Go on where?'

'I'm still waiting.'

'There's nothing to wait for.'

'You still haven't told me whether you saw him the night he died.'

'Haven't I? Are you sure?'

'Yes, I'm sure. Did you?'

'No, I didn't see him the night he died.'

'Why did it take so long?'

'Why did what take so long?'

'Giving a straight answer.'

'I'd already given you a straight answer, Plant. I told you, I last saw him a couple of days before.'

'Weren't you supposed to be seeing him the night he died?'

'Who says?'

'It doesn't matter who says.'

'I think it does,' she said.

She reached for her bag of tricks and produced her stash and began rolling a joint.

'Were you?'

'Was I what?'

'Were you supposed to be seeing him?'

'I don't know about supposed,' she said. 'What's "supposed" supposed to mean?'

'Had you made an arrangement?'

She ran her tongue along the gum of the rolling paper, provocative and pink, smiling up at him as she did so.

'Yes,' she said.

Plant sighed.

'Well, that's something.'

'What's something?'

'A straight yes.'

She lit the joint and took a couple of drags on it.

'Here,' she said, passing it across. 'Calm down. You're getting stressed out.'

He shook his head.

'You don't smoke on duty, is that it?'

'Something like that.'

'Well, tell me when you go off duty and I'll roll you another one.'

'Thank you.'

'My pleasure,' she said.

She stretched, languorously.

'And to think, it could be yours too.'

'What could be?'

'My pleasure.'

A pair of sea eagles circled above them, slow, powerful wing beats, wide sweeping orbits. Along the beach a couple of pelicans sunned themselves on the warm sand. Two brahminy kites perched on the dead tree. All nature was paired off, the two great sexes that interanimate the world.

'What was the arrangement?' he asked.

'What arrangement was that?'

Plant made a sort of hissing noise. Denoting exasperation.

'See, you are stressed.'

'Will you answer the question?'

'I don't believe I have to,' she said. 'I don't believe you have any statutory powers of inquisition. Am I correct in supposing that you don't?'

'Yes,' Plant said.

'Yes, what?' she said, like a mother correcting an impolite child.

'Yes, please,' he said.

She laughed.

'You are quite sweet,' she said. 'And if you got your gear off you might turn out to be quite attractive. Why don't you have a swim, Plant?'

'I'm not a swimmer,' he said.

'You can't swim?' she asked, a bit too eagerly, as if ascertaining whether it would be possible to drown him without any difficulty.

'I can but I don't.'

'As with so many other things.'

'No,' he said.

'Well,' she said, 'that's hopeful.'

She handed the joint across. He took it automatically and inhaled deeply.

'See,' she said, 'that wasn't so terrible, was it?'

He choked and coughed. But no, it wasn't so terrible.

'What else could you be persuaded to try?' she asked.

'Can we just get these questions answered?'

'And afterwards?' she said.

'What about afterwards?'

'Exactly my question,' she said. 'Do I get a reward or anything?'

'We'll see.'

'I wonder,' she said. 'But a girl lives in hope.'

'You'd arranged to meet Rock that night?'

'Yes.'

'And did you?'

'No.'

'What happened?'

'Nothing happened. He didn't show.'

'And?'

'And nothing.'

'Did you call him?'

'Of course not.'

'Why not?'

'And speak to the savage beast? "Excuse me, Mrs Richmond, do you have your husband there, he didn't turn up for the fuck he booked in for."'

'And where were you meeting him?'

'At my place.'

'Not at the lighthouse?'

'Why would I meet him at the lighthouse?'

'That's where he was found.'

'Why on earth would I want to meet him there when we could meet at my place?'

'So where's your place?'

'If you play your cards right I'll take you there.'

'Where?'

'You'll see.'

'Was there anyone with you?'

'With me?'

'Yes, with you.'

'No, why would there be? You think we were into group sex?'

'I've no idea what you're into.'

'Only one way to find out,' she said.

'So you were alone?'

'Would you prefer a group scene?' she said. 'Shall I call up a friend?'

'Just answer the question,' he said.

'I could say the same to you,' she said.

'There was no one with you?'

'No. I already said that. Pay attention, Plant.'

'So no one can give you an alibi.'

'No.'

'You just waited there.'

'Yes.'

'You didn't go out and meet him somewhere else?'

'And put a gun to his head? No, not that I recall. Is that what you think, Plant?'

'I don't know,' he said.

'Well, isn't that a reassuring answer?'

'Is it?'

She gave a tuneful little laugh.

'Is it all right if I go for a swim now?'

'Sure.'

'Sure you won't join me?'

'Sure.'

'What about afterwards? Come and check out my place and have that cup of coffee?'

'What cup of coffee?'

'The one you men of a certain age are always suggesting coming in for at the end of a date.'

'Why not?' he said.

'How gracious you are.'

'Is this a date?'

'I think so, don't you?' she said. 'Anyway, we can always make it one.'

She stood up and danced down to the waves, as light as air. The waves leapt up to embrace her. Plant could see why they might.

He rolled himself a joint from her stash while he waited. Out at sea the dolphins rose and plunged in joyful exhilaration. The gannets dived in ecstatic frenzy. The sea eagles circled, the pelicans took off like lumbering jumbo-jets, the brahminy kites began their patrol of the bushland bordering the beach. All nature was at play. Or preparing to catch fish.

Chapter 25

'Let's go then,' she said.

'Let's go where?'

'Just down the beach.'

'You got a coffee machine down the beach?'

She smiled. 'Plant,' she said, 'you do make a fuss.'

She began walking and he followed her. Like a poodle. Out at sea, on the far horizon, the Cape Byron lighthouse stood in priapic splendour.

'We're walking to Byron?' he asked.

'Just Ocean Shores.'

'That's miles.'

'It's not as far as Byron.'

'It's still miles.'

'Kilometres, we call them these days,' she said. 'It will keep you fit. Build up your stamina.'

'We can't walk to Ocean Shores.'

'I can,' she said.

He tagged along, expostulating.

'How do I get back?'

'The way you get there,' she said. 'Unless you've used up all your manhood by then. In which case, as a mark of satisfaction, I might drive you back.'

'Why can't we drive now?'

'Because my car's down there.'

'Mine isn't.'

'I don't take rides in cars with strange men,' she said. 'I'm a well brought-up girl.'

They got there. It took a good hour, and the sun was beating down hard. He gave up looking for shells and concentrated on walking. And on being encouraged. She encouraged him with little gestures. An arm around him momentarily. The re-wrapping of her sarong, with a glimpse of her breasts, so much more provocative than the full nakedness earlier on the beach. The toss of her head, suggestive, encouraging. On they went, along beside the Billinudgel Nature Reserve, on past Golden Beach and New Brighton. They didn't talk much. For his part Plant was saving his breath. Who knew what she was saving?

'I wouldn't have picked you for an Ocean Shores type,' he said.

'And what is an Ocean Shores type?'

He didn't in fact know. It was a totally new development, risen from the swamp, with reaches of the Brunswick River and bushland and modern three- and four-bedroom family homes. Suburbia beside the sea. And the stories of the CIA stake in its development.

'What would you have picked me as?'

'More Eureka,' he said, 'or Federal or maybe Nimbin.'

'A country hick.'

'Not exactly. A bit more alternative.'

'Daddy's generosity doesn't extend to encouraging my alternative propensities,' she said.

It was an extraordinarily anonymous house. Absolutely clean and bare and swept. It looked like she was all packed up and ready to leave at a moment's notice. Nothing belied its suburban exterior. Except perhaps its excess of sterility. Nothing proclaimed her personal touch. Whatever her personal touch might have been. For the moment it was Plant, as she helped him unbutton his shirt, his belt, his trousers. He found himself propelled into the bedroom, onto the bed. He surrendered to her irresistible force. Madimi might have been a spirit name. But she was a little demon in bed.

'Tell me about your work, Plant,' she said, afterwards.

'Are you pumping me?' he asked.

'You want another screw?' she asked. 'Or does your language always carry a sexual freight?'

'Sexual freight?'

'Sexual freight, sexual fright,' she said. 'Whatever gets your rocks off.'

'Gets your rocks off?' he said. 'I haven't heard that for years. Is that some phrase you learned from Rock Richmond?'

'You're not jealous of the dead, are you, Plant?'

'Was there anything to be jealous of?'

'What is that supposed to mean?'

'Was it a meaningful relationship, as they used to say in the seventies?'

'I don't know about the seventies,' she said. 'Rather before my time. But it was meaningful for me, yes. Brief as it was.'

'It was brief?'

'I thought I was asking you the questions.'

'Were you?'

'About your work.'

'My work?' he said. 'I suppose you could say this is my work.'

'Asking questions while getting laid?'

'So what is your work?' he asked.

'Oh, darling,' she said. 'This isn't work.'

'So what is it?'

'Well, it's hardly a meaningful relationship, yet, is it?'

'Do you work?'

'I'm just a remittance girl,' she said. 'Daddy pays the bills as long as I keep out of town.'

'Daddy?'

'Oh, you know.'

'A sugar daddy?'

'But no less real.'

'So you don't work?'

'You could say I was a free spirit,' she said.

'Does that mean you are? Or is it just something you could say?'

'Oh, Plant,' she said. 'I think you must have studied English Literature. In the old days. All that Close Analysis. Close Analysis and Dating, wasn't it?'

'How do you know about that?' he asked. 'That all went out years ago.'

'Pillow talk, I imagine,' she said. 'How I know about most things. I must have had an old tutor just like you.'

'Like me?'

'An older man who talked all the time. While doing it. And before. To say nothing of after.'

'And you don't?'

'I adapt,' she said. 'You want to talk, I'll talk. Tell me about your work, Plant. Do you think Maggie did it?'

The bare grey walls of the bedroom like a holding cell. The windows covered with grey plastic Venetian blinds, closed to the world. Built-in wardrobes, not even a timber cupboard or chest of drawers to soften the utilitarian functionalism of it all. No dressing table laden with unguents and the perfumes of the East. Just a single chair to toss clothes over, and the double bed, and Madimi.

'Did it?'

'Killed Rock.'

'Why would I think that?'

'I would have thought it was a natural conclusion,' she said.

'Seems pretty unnatural to me.'

'Fair enough. Doesn't mean she didn't do it.'

'Do you think she did?' he asked.

'Motive, means and opportunity,' she said.

'What motive?'

'Oh, jealousy, of course. And probably financial. Had she insured his life?'

'I've no idea.'

'Really, Plant,' she said. 'That's terribly remiss of you not to have found that out straight away.'

'She's my client. I'm not in the business of trying to incriminate my clients.'

'Not even a little bit? Not even for me?'

'Why for you?'

'I don't think she terribly likes me.'

'Well, that's explicable.'

'It doesn't make her a nice person.'

'No, I imagine you mightn't find her so.'

'But you do.'

'Find her a nice person? She's all right.'

'You've got a thing for dominatrices, have you?'

'Dominatrices?'

'Plural of dominatrix. Or is just one of them enough for you? Like the unfair Maggie.'

'I don't think so,' he said.

'But you're not sure?'

'I'm sure.'

'That's good. I wouldn't want to think you were weird.'

'Wouldn't you?'

'Not in that way, anyway,' she said.

'Men fear strong women.'

'Anyone you don't fear, Plant?'

He thought about it.

'That was a heavy thing to say.'

'And?' she said.

'And?'

'And what's the answer?'

'I refuse to be bullied into making a reply.'

'That's an interesting strategy.'

'Strategy?'

'Witty banter to avoid answering the question.'

Plant decided silence was the best way out of that one. She was quick. Very sharp. He had to admire the way she could handle a question-and-answer session. It reminded him of his own tricks of interrogation and evasion. As if she had done some other training course before enrolling in creative writing. Or had she just picked it up along the way? But along what way would that have been?

'So who do you suspect?'

'I'm not sure I suspect anybody at this stage.'

'Shouldn't you be out there suspecting someone?'

'I probably should,' he said. 'Except I seem to have got waylaid.'

'Waylaid,' she said. 'See what I mean about the sexual freight of your language.'

'Show me,' he said.

She showed him.

Chapter 26

Eureka was a pretty little settlement in the gently rolling hills, inland of Byron and Coolamon Scenic Drive. But the Eureka Rifle Club was nowhere near. It turned out to be up north in one of the reaches of the Tweed estuary, and it took its name not from Eureka village but from the event that had given Eureka village its name, the Eureka stockade, that historic armed uprising of the miners against civil authority back in Ballarat in 1854.

Plant tracked it down. There was an aluminium gate, much like his own, and similarly padlocked, with a notice attached to it saying 'Eureka Rifle Club Inc. Private Property. No Unauthorised Entry. Shoots alternate Saturday afternoons and Sunday morning.' Another notice proclaimed the endorsement of NSW Sport and Recreation. Behind the gate was a field, presumably the site of target practice. There was no sound of anyone firing at targets. Or at anything else. Inquiries were directed to the Australia First caravan park which bordered the field.

At the point where the rifle range and the caravan park adjoined a windsock hung limply from a white pole. White paint marked a circle on the mown grass. A sign announced 'Helicopter Emergency Landing Pad. Keep Clear.'

Plant drove down the road to the entrance to the Australia First Caravan Park. It was flanked with a Eureka Stockade flag and a Confederate Army flag. Hands across the ocean. A mud-spattered Land Rover was parked in the driveway, original olive drab. It sported an impressive array of aerials and roof mounted spotlights. Its front was protected by a substantial looking bull-bar. A spare wheel was mounted at the back, its cover proclaiming 'Special Operations (Vietnam) Association.' Another spare was mounted on the roof rack. A bumper sticker announced 'I Own a Gun and I Vote.' In the rear window a sticker with the Australian Flag advised 'Australia – Love It or Leave It.' Round the licence plate was the slogan 'I am a Vietnam Veteran. We were winning when I left.'

There was a Besser brick building like a blockhouse or a bunker. A sign above the door announced Office. Another sign instructed 'All Visitors to Site Report Here.' Rising high above the roof was a huge radio mast. It didn't look like something rigged up to listen to community FM.

Plant wondered. After all, the Eureka brigade and the Australia First movement and the Confederate army were not exactly loyalist episodes from the winning side. They were not the signs of a one hundred percent reliable sort of consciousness. Nor was it immediately apparent to Plant whether the Australia First Caravan Park was a progressive, green and environmentally-friendly site of the future, or a run-down relic of a receding past. Ancient though not yet historic caravans were parked amidst straggly casuarinas. Casuarinas were the native growth, but they were not the sort of tree that looked neat and orderly; they possessed an inherent, untameable straggliness. The high screen of bamboo running down the one side looked definitely yesteryear: no longer an acceptable, approved growth, usually destined for eradication as an alien by the ethnic-cleansing greenies. The vans were lined up in neat rows, but nonetheless they leaned and lurched somewhat, as if the reclaimed swamp they were parked on had subsided, or a high wind had swept through.

A notice nailed to a post instructed potential guests to report to the office before parking vans or pitching tents. Relocation is a pain, it promised. Further notices warned that lighting fires was prohibited. All of them were pock-marked with rifle fire.

A single magpie foraged amidst the grass. Up in one of the gums a couple of crows cawed. A six-foot long goanna lumbered across the track between two rows of vans, its tongue darting in and out, left and right, as it searched for prey.

The park was protected from the road by a shaggy jumble of bushes and trees of different kinds and different heights, tea-tree and eucalyptus and banksia, with pines reaching above them. No romantic looking palms. None of the trimmed box hedge or blooming bottle-brush. Nothing seemed to be blooming. It was not a place to attract the passing nuclear family to overnight. No prices were listed at the roadside, no inviting special rates. It did not actually declare 'No Vacancy,' but nor did it admit that accommodation might be available. It was not oriented towards the passing trade. It would have to depend on regulars, with their own vans permanently there for their weekend escapes. Swimming, fishing, bird watching, rifle shooting.

'Can I help you, sir?'

The man who emerged from the office was dressed in crisply pressed off-white trousers and ironed white shirt, short-sleeved, epaulettes. His brown shoes were highly polished. From the rows of ancient caravans and dusty casuarinas Plant had expected a hairy, singleted, shorts and football socks type. But not at all. This was immaculate, officer-class mufti. It seemed in marked contrast to the ramshackle park. But now that he looked at the park again, he realised the ramshackleness was only the superficial impression, contrived and preserved perhaps. A careful look revealed that it was in fact well maintained, the grass trimmed close along the tracks and around the casuarinas, no fallen branches or debris, nowhere for snakes to lurk. Nowhere for anything to lurk. It was just that the casuarinas looked scruffy and the caravans old. But that was the nature of casuarinas and old caravans. The more Plant looked at it, the more carefully contrived the ramshackle air appeared. The more it looked like camouflage. A carefully concealed base camp. Or was that a Fullalove style fantasy? Was it after all just somewhere time forgot, slowly sinking into the alluvial flat? It hardly looked like it would generate much of a living for anyone. No freezer with Paddle Pops and Weiss's ices. No Coca-Cola dispenser.

The man's smile was crisp beneath his trimmed, gingery moustache. His arms were red and freckled, not burned red but that red of the Norman, or the Norseman, Viking red, Crusader red, his red hair carefully trimmed en brosse. Clearly a lot of Mars in his chart. It was not at all what Plant had expected. He had fallen into the easy prejudice of expecting the surly, monosyllabic gruffness of the regimental sergeant major. Or the wired aggression of the psychopathic killer. Something to go along with those bumper stickers. And here was the modern military professional, all sweet reasonableness and mellifluous courtesy in a posh, private-school accent. The sort of chap who might even be diffident about military adventurism in the Middle East, far more reasonable than his political masters.

'If you have a moment,' Plant said, all sweet reasonableness too. He produced his card from his wallet, handed it across. 'I'm looking into the death of Rock Richmond,' he said.

'Thought I recognised you, saw you at the memorial service, tragic business.'

'Yes,' Plant said.

'Jake Illingworth,' he said, reaching out a freckled hand. A firm, dry handshake.

'And how can I help you?'

None of the, what's it got to do with me, squire?

'I believe you knew him.'

'From way back,' Jake said.

'From your commune days?'

'You've heard about that, have you? I imagine you would have if you've done your research and investigation. No, way before that. We were in the corps together.'

'The corps?'

'Officer Training Corps,' he said. 'Back at school.'

'You were at school with him?'

'Yes, we go way back. Went,' he corrected.

'I didn't realise that.'

'Well, why would you? Unless you were an old boy. We'd go down to reunion dinners once in a while.'

'Really.'

'Splendid bash. Black tie. Old school hall. Quite moving, really. Can't say they were the happiest days of my life, but they weren't bad. Not bad at all.'

'What were the happiest days of your life?'

'Ah, that would be telling. Vietnam. Vietnam was pretty

good. So was the commune. So's this. Can't complain about any of it. It's been a good life. And still more to come. Have to wait till the end to say which were the best years.'

'What about Rock?'

'What about him?'

'What were the best years for him?'

'Well, you'd have to ask him. Oh,' he checked himself, 'stupid of me. Can't get used to the fact that he's not with us any more. Still expect him to come dropping by. Have a yarn. Always good for a yarn, Rock. A born storyteller. I told him, you're wasted in journalism. Should've been a best-selling novelist. He tried, of course. Somehow it never happened for him.' He gazed out into the middle distance, brooding rather than focusing. 'Sorry, what was your question, what were the best years for him? Hard to say. I think they were all pretty good. Out on his board, probably. He loved to surf.'

'And shoot?'

'Oh, he'd bang away at target practice. But he was more your surfing sort of type. And music, of course. Loved his music. Not a bad voice. Heard him once or twice with that clergyman fellow, not bad, not bad at all. They were talking about cutting a record. Could've been a hit.'

'What about his history of the alternative?'

'That too. That was his other bet. Reckoned it was going to be a best-seller. Pity about that. Can't imagine we'll ever see it now.'

'It wasn't finished?'

'Shouldn't think so. He was still at the stage of talking to people. Chasing people up for interviews. Get it all down before they lost their memories, those that still had any. It was taking a lot of time to track them all down.

Lots of them had scattered. Of course he'd lived up here all through those years. But I don't think he'd got round to writing it down. He was looking for an angle.'

'An angle?'

'Something to make it all fresh. Not just your routine old regional history funded by the shire council. He wanted something to give it an edge.'

'Did he find it?'

'Ah, that I can't say. Funny types, these author fellows. They play their cards pretty close to their chest. He'd come round and talk to me about those days. He'd have his string of questions. But he never gave any clue to how it was all shaping up. I suppose that's the way they work. You'd have to be careful. Much like the army. Wouldn't want the enemy coming along and pinching your battle plan.'

'They did.'

'They did what?'

'His computer was stolen. And his files.'

'Were they now? That's pretty steep, I hope he has back-ups. Oh,' he said again, 'stupid me. It won't make any difference if he did, now, will it? Still can't get used to the fact he's no longer with us.'

He sniffed, sniffed and cleared his throat.

'Terrible business. Hard to believe, really. Not like him at all. But you never know. Was he ill, or something? Some chaps put a brave face on it. Then you find out they'd had some terrible illness they never told you about. Though he looked pretty fit to me.'

'He wasn't ill,' Plant said.

'Is that so? Then why did he do it?'

'It's possible that he didn't.'

Jake frowned. He gave a look of military puzzlement.

'You've lost me there,' he said.

'It's possible someone else did it.'

'Someone else did it? What, you mean someone shot him? He was murdered?'

'Could be.'

'Good lord,' he said. 'Good lord. Why would anyone do that?'

'That's what I'm trying to find out.'

'Good lord. And you're on the case?'

'Mrs Richmond hired me.'

'Maggie, well well. And what have you found out?'

'Not a lot,' Plant said.

'Well,' he said. 'Good lord. And you think I can help?'

'I'm talking to people who knew him.'

'Of course. Well, that would be the way to go. But murder. Really. It's hard to take in. I wish I could help. But really. It defies explanation. I can't imagine who would want to kill him.'

'That's the sort of thing I need to know.'

'What sort of thing is that?'

'That you can't imagine who would want to kill him.'

'Meaning what?'

'That he had no obvious enemies.'

'Ah, get you now. I see.'

'Tell me about the Eureka Rifle Club.'

'Tell you what?'

'Are you involved in it?'

'I'm the president, yes.'

'And what does it do?'

'What does it do? What do you think it does? It's a rifle club.'

'So you shoot?'

'Target practice, competitions. Why?'

Why indeed? This was Fullalove's obsession, militias, arms caches.

'Oh, I say, now come on, really,' Jake said. 'Just because Rock was shot that doesn't put the rifle club in the picture.'

'Not necessarily.'

'I should think not. It's an Olympic sport now, you know.'

'You've got some Olympians in the club?'

'Not quite. But some pretty good shots all the same, I'll say that.'

'They meet here.'

'In the target field.'

'Is there a clubhouse?'

'No, no, nothing like that. They just come here to keep up their training.'

'They stay in the caravans?'

'No, no, that's mainly fishermen. Been coming here for ages.'

'No one in the club who might have borne him a grudge?'

'I say, come on. No one else would know how to pull a trigger, is that it? Rock wasn't that regular a shooter. But when he came he got on with everyone. No tickets on Rock. You're barking up the wrong tree if you think anyone in the club would have been involved.'

'When was the last time he shot?'

'Not that long ago, actually. Brought that little bimbo of his along with him. Maddingley or whatever she calls herself.'

'Madimi.'

'Could be. Can't say I took to her. Ruthless little bitch in my opinion. Met too many of that type in the service. Absolutely ruthless. Kill you as soon as spit at you. But no accounting for taste. Maggie could be pretty ruthless too. He must have liked them like that. I tell you one thing, though, she might have looked like a bimbo but she was a cracker of a shot. Absolute bloody markswoman. One hundred percent professional. I wouldn't have minded her on my team.' He chuckled in admiration. 'Rather have her on my team than on the other side, that's for sure.'

'What's it take to be a good marksman? Or woman?' Plant asked.

'A good eye, coordination, concentration. Keeping cool under fire.'

'And ruthlessness?'

'Oh, absolutely. Especially if you're out there in the field. Not much point being sentimental if you're trained as a sniper.'

Plant figured he hadn't been referring to the target field.

'By the way, how did you know Rock was shot?'

'Wasn't he?'

'Yes, he was.'

'Just seemed to know it. Don't ask me how. In the papers, probably. Or somebody might have said something. Everyone seems to say he was shot. People just assumed he'd shot himself. Which I must say, never seemed likely to me. That's why I wondered if he'd had some, you know, sickness.'

'He wasn't depressed?'

'Not that I noticed. But it's not important whether he was or he wasn't, is it, if someone else shot him?'

'True enough.'

'So why would somebody want to shoot him?'

'That's what I'm trying to find out,' Plant said.

'Well, good luck. If you need any help, give me a call. Hope you get the bastard. Look, if I think of anything I'll give you a call. Without fail. Need a bit of time to take it on board. Don't know what I can come up with. But I've got your card, where did I put it now? If I think of something I'll let you know. And feel free to ask again if you need to know anything. Only too ready to help if there's anything I can do.'

He reached out his hand again to shake goodbye.

It would have seemed churlish to have persisted with any more questions. And like Jake Illingworth, Plant felt the need to go away and sit down and think through what he had been told. If anything.

Had Jake deftly brought the interview to an end? Or was it a matter of being shocked and flustered? Did military chaps get shocked and flustered at the news of shootings? Or under fire? No doubt some did and some didn't. Perhaps he should check out Jake's military record and see if he had won any medals. Or maybe his line had been interrogating captured insurgents and he knew all about evasion.

'He pulled the wool over your eyes,' Fullalove said.

'It's not impossible,' Plant conceded.

'Not impossible? It's a certainty, mate. Those officer-class types, they know how to do it, they've all done their time jackarooing. Once you've handled a merino ram, someone like you is just a sacrificial lamb to the slaughter.'

'Thank you,' Plant said.

'Nothing personal,' Fullalove said. 'You just don't have

the weight or the firepower. He'd see you coming and spit on his hands with delight.'

'I don't see him as the sort who spits on his hands.'

'Metaphorically,' Fullalove said.

Plant grunted. Even to himself it sounded suspiciously like a bleat.

'You should've taken me along.'

'And what would you have done?' Plant asked. 'Slammed him against the wall and asked if he was running a private army?'

'There's a time for questions and a time for action,' Fullalove said.

'And which is this?'

'I'll let you know,' Fullalove said. 'I'm going to check him out. I might stay there for a couple of nights. Hire a van.'

'Sounds like a good idea,' Plant agreed.

What bliss! The house to himself again. He could even invite Madimi over. What bliss indeed.

'Yes, I think you should do that.'

Fullalove looked at him suspiciously.

'I should have thought of it myself,' Plant added.

'You should've.'

'But I didn't.'

'Nobody's perfect,' Fullalove grinned, his evil, missing-toothed grin.

Plant grinned along with him.

Happy days are here again. Or soon will be.

Chapter 27

Plant decided to take the opportunity to meet Uncle Toby while Fullalove was occupied. Some conversations were best held on a need-to-know basis. Most conversations, indeed, that involved either Uncle Toby or Fullalove. And since Uncle Toby had made the suggestion of meeting for lunch, back at the wake, it was likely to be for something in the need-to-know area. Whether it was Uncle Toby's need, or Plant's, Plant was not sure. At an informed guess, he assumed it would be the former. But it wouldn't hurt to get an idea of Uncle Toby's needs. They might well be something Plant needed to know.

Uncle Toby lived up on the Gold Coast in a glitzy penthouse overlooking the ocean. High enough to survive the highest tsunami.

'Omeros at noon,' he instructed when Plant phoned. 'Marina Mirage, Main Beach.'

'Omeros?'

'Homer to you. As in the *Iliad*.'

'I always preferred the *Odyssey*,' Plant said.

'I'm sure you did, dear boy. Sex and drugs rather than war and honour. Fish all right?'

'Fish?'

'Your vegetarianism extends to fish, does it?'

'Well ...'

'Good for the brain, as they have yet again rediscovered. Especially for growing children.'

'I can stretch a point,' Plant offered.

Fish oil was good for muscle tone, too. He had a feeling he might have a need for both increased brainpower and muscle tone.

'Nowhere like Australia for fish and seafood,' Uncle Toby said. 'Parts of the Mediterranean are quite fished out. I know the good doctor said patriotism was the last resort of a scoundrel, but really, we are such a lucky country.'

'For fish-eaters,' Plant agreed.

'Not just for fish-eaters,' Uncle Toby insisted.

Uncle Toby was sitting there resplendent in Bombay bloomers and long socks and some sort of short-sleeved safari shirt, all pockets and buttons and tags and shoulder straps. And a money pouch worn around his waist, marsupial fashion. Instead of a pith helmet he sported a rakish panama.

'I thought we might sit outside,' he said, sitting there in one of the cane and metal chairs.

The tables were ranked along the wooden boardwalk beside the marina. Uncle Toby had chosen one at the water's edge, a quiet corner, the sort of spot you might choose if you preferred not to be overheard, and with the ambient noise of the sea and the powerboats and the tourist cruisers making audio-surveillance more difficult. Or maybe he just didn't like being close to other people much.

'Fine,' Plant agreed.

'More relaxing,' Uncle Toby added, gesturing at the luxury cruisers. The soothing effects of wealth and conspicuous consumption.

'Glad you called. Much easier to have a little talk up

here than at the funeral. Away from that dreadful widow woman. I never knew what poor Richmond saw in her. Puffed up with opinion like a Haitian blowfish. Exuding ignorance like a cuttlefish squirting ink. I used to adore risotto nero, but she has quite put me off it.'

He dabbed his lips with a napkin.

'But let us put all that behind us. How do you like it here? I find it reminds me of happy days in the Mediterranean.'

'Greek memories,' Plant suggested.

'Compton Mackenzie,' Uncle Toby said. 'Absolutely.'

'Compton Mackenzie?'

'The title of one of his books. I thought you were alluding to it.'

'No,' Plant said. 'What's it about?'

'Spying,' Uncle Toby said.

'Of course,' Plant said. 'You knew him in Greece?'

'A bit before my time, dear boy. He was out there in World War I.'

'Ah well,' Plant said, 'I'm sure nothing much has changed.'

'I am sure you are right,' Uncle Toby agreed.

The waiter came up and Uncle Toby suggested a South Australian Riesling.

Plant cast his eye down the wine list. The recommended Riesling was at the bottom of the price range. He had no objection to that. It was never a free lunch with Uncle Toby. Always a matter of paying your own share.

'Why not?' Plant said.

'Why not indeed?'

'Fine,' Plant agreed.

'Are you keeping busy?' Uncle Toby asked when the waiter had gone. As if checking on Plant's ability to pay.

'Busy enough.'

'And how busy is busy enough? Enough for a busy bee or more suited to a drone?'

'There's a lot to be said for a drone's life,' Plant said.

'Suitably funded.'

'Suitably funded,' Plant agreed.

'The good old days of tenure and a job for life.'

'I never knew them,' Plant said.

'They weren't to be sniffed at,' Uncle Toby said. 'But you survive,' he added.

'Oh, I survive,' Plant said.

It was the sort of statement, he realised as soon as he had made it, that it was best not to make. It was tempting Providence. Or, if not Providence, the dark forces. Possibly dark forces known to Uncle Toby and Compton Mackenzie. The sort of forces that might have been wondering if it was such a good thing that he was surviving, and considering action to produce an alternative outcome.

'I hear you were doing some work for poor Richmond,' Uncle Toby said.

'How did you hear that?' Plant asked.

'Through my ears, I imagine,' Uncle Toby said. 'The customary way.'

'Did Maggie Richmond tell you?'

Uncle Toby gave his impression of a man suppressing a shudder.

'Oh no, she never tells me anything.'

'Really.'

'Insufferable opinionated woman. Blissed out on ignorance. Strictly between you and me. I wouldn't want to seem unfriendly in her current circumstances. Bereavement,' he added, in case Plant had forgotten.

'But in any other circumstances?' Plant suggested.

'I can't imagine what they might possibly be. I rather hope there aren't any.'

'So she didn't tell you.'

'No, she certainly did not.'

But he did not say who did. Maybe Rock had told him. Maybe he had other sources of information. Without a doubt he had. And he wasn't saying.

'Poor Richmond had some problem, I understand.'

Plant nodded.

'Something about a burglary.'

Plant nodded again.

'I gather he lost his computer and his files.'

Plant grunted agreement.

'Did he ever get them back?'

'No.'

'Was he upset?'

Plant tried a shrug.

'He gave no sign?'

'I didn't know him well enough to say. I imagine he was upset. But he didn't go on about it.'

'Any idea who did it?'

Plant was tempted to say 'No, have you?' but thought better of it. He shook his head again, instead.

'Not a clue?'

'Not a clue.'

'And now it turns out he's been murdered.'

'Yes,' Plant agreed.

'Any idea who might have done it?'

'No,' Plant said. 'Have you?' he added, unable to resist it this time.

'Apart from his wife? No, not at all.'

'You think his wife might have? His widow, that is,' he corrected himself.

'I would think she would be capable.'

'Anyone else?'

'No need to look any further, I should have thought.'

'How about Madimi Dee?' Plant suggested. To see what reaction it might elicit.

'And who is she?'

'I thought she might have been one of yours.'

'One of mine?'

'One of your girls.'

'I haven't had too many girls.'

'How many is too many?' Plant asked.

'Enough is enough,' Uncle Toby said.

He gestured to the waiter to come over and save them. The waiter obliged. Uncle Toby ordered whole snapper grilled. And vegetables. Plant ordered whiting fillets in batter. He felt bad about eating fish, taking life, but he liked the batter, even if it was said to be bad for you. Now he could feel doubly bad.

Chapter 28

'Who is this strangely-named person?' Uncle Toby asked when the waiter was safely back inside relaying their order.

'She was a friend of Rock Richmond's.'

'Just of poor Richmond's?' asked Uncle Toby. Keenly, Plant felt. 'Or a little friend of all the world?'

Plant shrugged. 'You know her?' he asked

'I think I already said no.'

'So your money's on Maggie.'

'Jealousy can be a powerful motive. And if this friend was what I think you mean by calling her a friend ...'

'You think it was personal.'

'What else would it be, dear boy?'

'Work related, maybe.'

'Was poor Richmond doing that much work? Surely he had no need to with that wealthy wife.'

'He was writing a book.'

'He was always writing a book,' Uncle Toby said. 'But I have never thought writing a book was really work.'

'What do you see it as?' Plant asked.

'More like an indulgence,' Uncle Toby beamed. 'I can't imagine anyone would want to kill poor Richmond because he was writing a book. Not even the severest of critics.'

The waiter came over with the wine. Uncle Toby examined the bottle, checked the vintage against the date in the wine list and nodded. He kept silent as the waiter opened it and poured out a sample. Then he went through the performance of testing it, sniffing the bouquet, taking a taste and rinsing it round his palate. He swallowed and nodded again. The waiter filled their glasses. Plant waited until they were alone again before continuing.

'Could he have discovered something?' he asked.

'I don't think he wrote that sort of book.'

'What sort of book?'

'Discoveries. He wasn't a scientific type.'

'I was thinking more of revelations.'

'Nor was he religious,' Uncle Toby offered.

'What sort did he write?'

'I'm sure you have looked at them as thoroughly as I,' Uncle Toby said, 'in the course of your investigations. And if you haven't, then perhaps you should. Help keep his memory green.'

'I'll make a point of it.'

'I think you'll find them pretty innocuous. Certainly hardly the sort of thing worth taking the poor boy's life over.'

Out on the marina the occasional powerboat ran its engine for a while. None of them seemed to move from their mooring. A canal-cruise boat idled at the jetty, taking on passengers. It was one of those calm, idyllic sunny days. And here we are, Plant reflected, talking about murder. Or if not quite talking about it, fencing around its edges.

'You didn't find the computer?'

'No,' Plant said. 'Nor the files. Nor any lead on who might have taken them or why.'

They sipped at the Riesling until the waiter returned with their order. Uncle Toby set to work at once dissecting his snapper, skilfully separating the flesh from the bones.

'Are you still looking?'

'No,' Plant said. 'Not a lot of point.'

'But you had been?'

'Not really. Rock just wanted the media alerted in case the material turned up.'

'And did it?'

Plant shook his head.

'And now you're working on the murder.'

'You keep well-informed,' Plant said.

A helicopter came in low and hovered noisily alongside the wharf. Uncle Toby glanced up at it.

'Keeping you under observation,' he said with a chuckle. He didn't indicate whether he was referring to himself or to the helicopter. The uses of ambiguity. The helicopter was an old Sikorski S-51. Hardly the latest thing in surveillance activity but probably adequate enough. Like Uncle Toby. It was black and unmarked and, hovering there, had a certain malevolent quality. Like Uncle Toby, again.

'Maggie gave me a watching brief to nose around. She felt the police were not keeping her informed.'

'Probably because they suspect her,' Uncle Toby said.

'That's what she felt.'

'As well she might.'

'You really think she might have done it?'

'Have you got a better suspect?'

'I don't have any suspects.'

Uncle Toby sat back with a smile and raised his glass.

'Here's to happy hunting,' he said.

Plant joined in the toast. It was only after he had taken his sip that he realised it had not been specified who was doing the hunting and who was being hunted.

'Did you ever go hunting with Rock?' he asked.

'Hunting? Hunting what, dear boy?'

'Anything,' Plant said. 'Rabbits. Hares. Kangaroos. Wallabies. Did he ever take you shooting?'

'Shooting? As with guns?'

'Yes. As with guns.'

'Dear boy, whatever gave you that idea? Do I look like I go shooting? I haven't held a gun in years. Dirty, noisy, smelly things.'

'You're more the unarmed combat type?'

Uncle Toby chuckled. 'You flatter me,' he said. He raised a hand up as if he were about to slice through the table in demonstration of his skills, but simply took another sip of the wine.

'But you held a gun in the past.'

'Way back in my youth.'

'When did you last hold a gun?' Plant asked. 'As a matter of interest.'

'Probably when I did my National Service.'

'You did National Service?'

'Oh yes. We all did in those days.'

'What in?' Plant asked. As if Uncle Toby were going to say, 'Intelligence Corps.'

'The University Regiment,' Uncle Toby said.

'So you know how to shoot.'

'This is part of your nosing around, is it? You're eliminating suspects, I take it. At least I hope you are eliminating them. You don't think I would have shot poor Richmond.'

Plant smiled.

'Just getting some idea of how many people he knew who knew how to use a gun.'

'And are there many?'

'Apart from you?' Plant said. 'I don't know.'

'I can assure you it wasn't me,' Uncle Toby said.

'I imagine that's what they'll all say,' Plant said.

'Well, really,' Uncle Toby said.

But he seemed remarkably undisturbed by the possibility that Plant had thought it might have been him. As if retired professors were regularly suspected of murdering their former students. Perhaps they were. Perhaps they regularly did murder them. It was the sort of thing that Fullalove might have the figures on.

'I don't see you as a trigger man,' Plant reassured him.

But that didn't mean he might not have been involved. And if he weren't involved, why had he wanted to have lunch? Was he perhaps a bit short of company in his retirement? Missing companionship and gossip. But could a man who chose to holiday in Kazakhstan really be retired?

'So what's your next move?' Uncle Toby asked.

'Some more tartare sauce,' Plant said, trying to catch the waiter's eye.

He succeeded, and Uncle Toby fell silent until they were alone again.

'Or is that classified?' he asked.

'Classified? Like an advertisement?' Plant said.

'Is your next move a secret not to be shared?'

'Not at all.'

Why was it, Plant reflected, that so many of the people he tried to question ended up questioning him? Could it be his fault, failing to retain control of the conversation? His incompetence? Or their anxieties? He hesitated to attribute guilt to them. They could hardly all be guilty. But they certainly all evinced anxiety. Unless it was innocent curiosity. He looked across at Uncle Toby, munching peas and potatoes. No, there was nothing innocent about Uncle Toby's curiosity.

'I just keep asking around,' Plant said, 'until somebody admits they did it. Unless the police get there first.'

'Is that likely?'

'That the police will get there first? Yes.'

'No, is it likely that someone will admit to doing it?'

'No, not really.'

'So you don't expect to be successful?'

'You win some, you lose some,' Plant said. When in doubt resort to cliché.

Uncle Toby carried on chewing.

'How hopeful are you?'

'Well,' Plant said. 'I don't want to seem to be taking Mrs Richmond's money under false pretences.'

'I shouldn't worry about that,' Uncle Toby said. 'She has plenty. And she can always get more. I don't think you need worry about her.'

'Maybe,' Plant said. 'And I don't want to self-incriminate.'

'Self-incriminate? You're not saying you shot him.'

'No, and I'm also not saying I'm not hopeful. That would be bad for business. Negative advertising.'

'Oh, I don't know,' Uncle Toby said. 'Some people might be more than happy to hire someone who wasn't hopeful. Make it look like they care and ensure nothing is discovered.'

'You really think Mrs Richmond would do that?'

'That I can't say,' he said. 'But if I were you, I wouldn't have too many worries about false pretences.'

'Right,' Plant said.

'So are you hopeful?'

Plant gave it his best shot. 'Not really,' he said.

He hoped Uncle Toby would believe him.

'Not at all, to be honest,' he added.

'Ah, honest Iago,' smiled Uncle Toby. 'Did you ever read Empson's essay on Honesty in *Othello*? A classic piece. So many meanings to such a simple word.'

Afterwards, Plant realised that Uncle Toby had not asked what was the subject of the book Rock Richmond had been writing. That might mean that he knew. But there again, that was not exactly sinister. Rock might have told him. It had certainly not been a secret if Madimi and Jake Illingworth and Max had all known. Even Maggie seemed to have known its general subject, while managing to keep the specifics at a distance.

Chapter 29

'I had lunch with Uncle Toby,' Plant said.

'The plot thickens,' Fullalove said.

'That's what I thought.'

'How does he fit in?'

'I'm not sure that he does. Except he was at the wake and he asked me to call him.'

'Maybe he liked your boyish complexion,' Fullalove said.

'Thank you,' Plant said.

'What was his interest?'

'Rock was one of his boys. Whatever that means. It could be just a personal interest.'

'Never.'

'Or if it is militia stuff ...'

'Of course it is.'

'Then maybe whoever Uncle Toby's wired up with was involved, or even if it's not his outfit, maybe they still got wind of it and he's got some sort of watching brief.'

'Was he warning you off?'

'Could have been. It's hard to say, he can be pretty oblique.'

'Letting you know he knows.'

'Possibly. Though what does he know?'

'He knows that you're nosing around. So he's probably letting you know things might get tricky if you start digging too deep. Tricky for you, that is.'

'Could be.'

'You see him as a hit man?' Fullalove asked.

'Uncle Toby?' Plant laughed. 'No.'

'You sure? Remember Chuck Burris?'

'Can't say I do.'

'American television producer and songwriter who did game shows. The Dating Game. The Gong Show. He had a day job as a CIA hit man.'

'Really? Is that true?'

'So he claimed. They made a movie of it. What more do you want?'

'I have trouble seeing Uncle Toby in quite that category.'

'As hit man or song writer?'

'He doesn't fit my picture of a hit man.'

'Somebody killed your client.'

'I don't think it was Uncle Toby.'

'You never can tell,' Fullalove said. 'It needs a certain sort of personality to be able to kill.'

'What sort?'

'Remorseless. Conscienceless. Sociopaths. I reckon he'd fit. Or they might have drugged and hypnotised him.'

'Why would they do that?'

'That's what they used to do, according to Chuck Burris. The idea was you'd hypnotise someone, give them a second identity, or a third, and then send them off as a courier or a killer. Since they didn't consciously know what they'd been programmed to do, there was no way they could be successfully interrogated if they got caught. Uncrackable.'

'Like the Manchurian candidate?'

'That's the idea,' Fullalove said. 'It's been done before. And if it's been done once, they're not going to stop doing it. Not if it works.'

'Are you serious?'

'Sure I'm serious. You want me to give you the references? There's a fair bit been written about it.'

'I mean about Uncle Toby. I don't see him as a hit man. Hypnotised or not.'

'Maybe he's the hypnotist. And old Rock Richmond was the assassin. Travelling the world and assassinating people. Uncle Toby would drive down to Byron, wave his manicured hands in front of Rock's innocent blue eyes, and pow. Off you go, Rock. Maybe that's what the book was about.'

'You really think so?'

'Or your caravan park man, Jake Illingworth. He'd be perfect. Trained to obey orders. Classic hypnotism subject.'

'Nice idea,' Plant said.

'It's foolproof. Why not keep on doing it? Uncle Toby's interested enough to get you to have lunch with him. Which means he's involved somewhere along the line. Has to be.'

'I still don't see him as the killer. Not for a moment.'

'So who did it?'

'He was very keen to suggest it was Rock's wife. A personal thing.'

'That would be right,' Fullalove said. 'That's what they'll say it is in the end. Something personal. And if they can't frame the wife they'll frame someone else. Assuming she didn't do it, of course.'

'I don't think she did,' Plant said. 'Not since Uncle Toby's so keen to suggest she did.'

'You wouldn't have a personal interest in this?'

'What sort of personal interest?'

'Some sort of involvement. Covering up for the old lady.

I notice from the way you talk about her lately you've been getting pretty chummy. Or is it just unrequited desire.'

'Not at all,' Plant said.

'Not at all chummy or not at all unrequited or not at all covering up for her?'

'Tell me,' Plant said, 'what's your interest in all this?'

'Oh, you know me,' Fullalove said.

'Sometimes I wonder if I do,' Plant said.

'While you were off eating fish with Uncle Toby I checked Jake Illingworth out,' Fullalove said.

'And?'

'Very fishy too. Claimed he hadn't got a vacancy. Every van booked. Fishing carnival, he said. Whatever that might be.'

'Some sort of competition. It's the sort of place fishermen go to. Hard to imagine who else would.'

'Forget fish,' Fullalove said. 'It's a meet.'

'A meat?'

'I'm going to stake it out.'

'Steak?'

'Then I'll grill the bastard.'

'Am I hearing you right?' Plant asked. 'You're planning some barbecue or something?'

'Something like that.'

'When?'

'When I'm ready. I think we're onto something, mate. It's a muster. I guarantee they'll be out there shooting beer bottles and doing unarmed combat with each other. All in their jungle greens. Or maybe desert gear these days. Be fascinating to find out.'

'And what's that got to do with Rock Richmond's

murder?'

'That's what we're going to find out, aren't we?'

'Are we?'

'Not a doubt in my mind,' Fullalove said. 'So are you in or out?'

'Am I in or out of what?'

'You coming along?'

'To stake out the rifle club?'

Fullalove nodded.

'He's already seen me,' Plant said.

'He's seen me, too.'

'But he knows I'm on the Richmond case.'

'You want out, is that what you're saying?'

'I think so.'

'You got a date with little Tinkerbell?'

'Could have.'

Fullalove shook his head dubiously.

'You sure that's such a good idea?'

'Seems like a good idea to me,' Plant said.

'What about the widow?'

'I'm not sure she's attracted to me in that sort of a way.'

'You can always find out. What makes you think little Tinkerbell is?'

'Empirical evidence.'

Fullalove chuckled sardonically.

'Don't say I didn't warn you.'

'You take care, too,' Plant said.

'I shall return.'

'But you may be some little time,' Plant said.

And indeed he was.

Chapter 30

The answering machine was flashing its little red light. Plant pressed its buttons and it delivered its angry message.

'Plant, where the hell are you, why don't you have a mobile? Phone me, fuck you.'

One of the reasons he didn't give out his mobile number was so that people couldn't reach him with angry messages whenever they felt like it and wherever he was. But he didn't think Mrs Richmond really wanted to know his reasons. Hers was more your rhetorical kind of question.

He called her back and she complained bitterly.

'Jake Illingworth has been round asking all these impertinent questions. Did you put him up to this, Plant?'

'Me? No, why would I put him up to it?'

'Because you're too chicken to ask yourself.'

'Ask what?'

'Did I do it?'

'Did you do what?'

'Kill Rock, of course.'

'Did you? Didn't I already ask you?'

She swore. Her years of representing the criminal classes had given her a rich vocabulary of vituperation, blasphemy and obscenity. Quite a thesaurus. Worth taping and publishing. Maybe he should provoke her again when he had the tape running and a publisher's contract.

'Only asking,' Plant said, when she'd finished.

She hadn't finished. She began again.

'Get round here,' she said, when she'd finished.

He got himself round there. She was looking quite fetching, less like a barrister and more Byron Bay like, summery and sub-tropical, all hibiscus and bird of paradise flowers in a light cotton fabric, and expensive.

'Tell me,' he said.

'Would you like a drink first?'

'Good idea,' he said.

Her mood seemed to have changed dramatically. Gone were the rage and the rodomontade, replaced by smiling consideration and sweet conciliation. Plant was happy to keep it that way, even if it meant having a drink.

'Champagne all right?' she said. Said rather than asked.

It wasn't really. It usually gave him a headache.

'It's the real thing,' she said, 'it won't give you a headache.'

She was getting psychic as well as charming.

'Celebrating?' he asked.

'What would I celebrate?' she asked. She gave him a steady, piercing look. 'Tell me, Plant, is there anything here to celebrate? Do I have cause for hope?'

He could feel himself beginning to blush beneath her gaze. Not since his schooldays had anyone managed to have that effect on him. It was one of the reasons he had worked on cultivating impassivity, so as not to blush. He could imagine what it was like in the dock, cross-examined by her.

'A satisfied client gave me a case of it,' she said, pouring the champagne into a couple of Waterford crystal glasses.

'Very nice.'

'That's what he thought. He was facing ten to fifteen years.'

'And you got him off.'

'Of course I got him off, Plant. I'm good.'

'I've never doubted you were good.'

'Well, Jake Illingworth does.'

'Tell me,' he said again.

'He clearly thinks I'm absolutely wicked. He invited himself round and inveigled his way in. I thought he was going to mumble on about commiserations and condolences and he starts interrogating me.'

'Interrogating?'

'No other word for it. And believe me, I've seen enough of it to know. Done enough, too.'

'Karma,' Plant said.

'Shut up, Plant, and listen. He starts quizzing me about the night Rock was killed and had I expected it and where was I exactly and did I have any witnesses to my movements. Damn cheek. I asked him what he thought he was doing. He said he'd been talking to you.'

She looked at him, expectantly.

'I did go to see him.'

'He said he was working for you.'

'No way,' Plant said.

'No way?'

'No way. He just offered to help me with my inquiries.'

'Whatever that means.'

'I took it to mean that he'd let me know if he happened to hear anything. '

'And you're sure you didn't send him round to me?'

'Sure I'm sure. Why would I?'

'He said he was working with you.'

'Really?'

'Implied.'

'Well, he might've implied it but he certainly isn't. If

anything he's one of my suspects.'

'And I'm one of his. Isn't that cosy. It just needs you to be one of my suspects and the circle would be complete, wouldn't it?'

'I suppose it would.'

'Suppose,' she snorted. 'I'd like to have you in court one day and sort you out. Why can't you ever say what you think in a straightforward way, Plant?'

'Maybe because I don't always know what I think.'

'"Maybe." There you are again. Mr Hypothetical. Is it a hypodermic, is it a hippopotamus, no, it's Plant, it's a hypothetical.'

'Possibly,' he said.

'Drink to it,' she said.

He obeyed. They clinked glasses and drank and she topped them up.

'Not getting a headache?' she asked.

'No.'

'Sure?'

'Sure.'

'Good. So where was I? Jake. You think Jake might have done it?'

'I don't know. Tell me what he said.'

'He just asked all this stuff in an insinuating way. Then he went on about the missing memory-stick. I thought we'd finished with all that. But no, he wanted to go through it all. Were there back-ups? What were Rock's plans? Had he said anything about the book in his will? Who was his literary executor? Was I going to have someone to finish the book? Why wasn't I going to?'

'So had he come round to quiz you about Rock's death or about the book?'

'Hard to say. A bit of both. He claimed they'd been working on the book together. He said he'd been feeding Rock the information and Rock had been writing it up. Or down.'

'Do you believe that?'

'I have no idea.'

'You and Rock never discussed the book?' Plant asked.

'Rock might have. I don't recall listening.'

'Would Rock have discussed it with Jake?'

'He could have. They were old mates. Jake said they were doing it as a last fling. A hot property was how he described it. You visited him. You've seen his caravan park. Do you think he's the sort of person who'd know a hot property?'

'So what did he want?'

'He seemed to want to know if there were back-up files.'

'Did you tell him?'

'I didn't tell him anything.'

'Why did he want them?'

'He said it was important the book should appear.'

'But you didn't give him the material.'

'I can't say I terribly like him, Plant. Too red and hairy. Apart from which he was never very friendly to me. I think he always resented me. Thought I was a bad influence on Rock. If you want to know the truth ...'

'Yes,' Plant said. 'Always.'

'I think he was jealous of me. He was in love with Rock. Like he was a reincarnated Knights Templar. Two buggers on a horse together. You know those military types. '

Plant made one of his grunting noises.

'Come over here,' she said. She patted the couch beside her. 'I can't hear you when you mumble to yourself like that.'

'Sorry,' Plant said.

'Don't apologise, just get over here.'

He picked up his glass and joined her. She topped it up.

'Are you living with anyone, Plant? Do you realise I don't know anything about you? Are you married or anything?'

'No.'

'A singular man.'

'I live alone,' he said.

Fullalove was only a temporary imposition, after all. Pray that it was so.

'Don't you ever get lonely?'

'Now and then,' he said.

'And is this now or then?' she asked.

He tried the non-committal again.

'See, you're mumbling. You must learn to speak up, young man.'

She picked up the bottle only to find with surprise that it was empty. She went out to the kitchen and Plant heard her pop open another one. She came back in with it and filled her glass. Plant put his hand across the top of his.

'I'd better not have any more.'

'What do you mean, you'd better not have any more? Why not? There's another whole case of the stuff out there. You don't expect me to have to drink it all on my own.'

'I'm driving.'

'Driving? Where do your reckon you're driving to?'

'Well, home.'

'Why are you doing that? You don't have to do that, Plant. You can spend the night here.'

'It's all right.'

'What do you mean, it's all right? It's not all right at all.'

'I'd better go.'

'Why? Don't you like me, Plant?'

'Yes, I like you.'

'But.'

'No buts.'

'So what's the problem? I'm too old for you, is that it? You prefer little teeny boppers like that sleazy Salome creature.'

'Madimi,' he said.

'Stop it. I don't ever want to hear her name again. So tell me I'm not too old for you.'

'You're not too old for me. Not at all.'

'Sure?'

'Sure.'

'So what's the problem?'

'I make it a policy not to get involved with clients.'

'Clients?' she said, 'is that what I am to you? A client? I thought we were friends, Plant.'

She reached out and held onto his hand.

'You did hire me.'

'Did I?'

'Yes.'

'And that's a problem.'

'It can be.'

'Right then,' she said. 'That's it, Plant. You're fired.'

'Fired?'

'As of now. You're off the case.'

'What for?'

'What does it matter what for? Insubordination. Refusing to take orders.'

'You're joking,' he said.

'No, I'm not. I've never been more serious. Now I'm not your client you can screw me. If you play your cards right I might even think about hiring you again. Eventually.'

'My cards?'

'Just do it, Plant,' she said. 'You can talk about suing for wrongful dismissal later.'

'Do it?'

'Yes, do it,' she said. 'I assume you do know how. Or do I have to spell out the details?'

She began unbuttoning him.

'I think I've got the general idea,' he said, accepting the inevitable. As the Chinese proverb puts it, when confronted by an irresistible force, lie back and enjoy it.

'There,' she said, 'that wasn't so terrible, was it?'

'Not at all,' Plant said. 'Rather good, actually.'

'"Rather good, actually." You certainly know how to whisper sweet nothings in a woman's ear.'

'A ripper,' he said.

'That's better. See, when you put your mind to it, you can manage.'

'More than manage,' he said.

'Is that so?' she said. 'So let's try you again, Plant. Make sure you're not just all talk.'

'Whatever you say,' he said.

'That's what I like to hear,' she said. 'Unemployment suits you, Plant, did you know that?'

'Is this what was called an ethical dilemma?' Plant asked himself. Without a doubt Mrs Richmond was an obvious suspect. He had to think of her as Mrs Richmond in this context, Maggie was too ... He searched for a convenient word but there was only one that applied: intimate. He could see why he had a rule of not sleeping with clients or their partners. How could you suspect someone you were sleeping with? Or had slept with: there was no necessary expectation this was going to be an on-going thing. Or, more to the point, you might well suspect them, but how could you actively investigate them? But how could he have actively investigated her, anyway? She was his client. Had been, at least. She hadn't hired him to incriminate her. Of course, she might have hired him to prevent his incriminating her. That was another ethical dilemma, too, probably. But until the police came investigating him, he would let that one rest.

Then it struck him that she was no longer his client. She had fired him. That left him free to suspect her. And investigate her, too. But if she was no longer his client, who was? Nobody. So who would finance the inquiries? Nobody. So what was there in it for him? Nothing. Except the thrill of the chase. He could do without that. He would leave that to Fullalove. In the meantime, fired, what was he to do?

'Plant, come over here,' she ordered.

The simplest thing was to do what he was told.

Chapter 31

Plant had always appreciated the way that Byron Bay's original street names commemorated poets and playwrights. He made a point of trying to recall their work as he walked along the streets named after them. Henry Lawson, poet of the people.

'But not until a city feels Red Revolution's feet

Shall its sad people miss awhile the terrors of the street.'

Unfashionable sentiments, but not without their appeal. For a moment late in the nineteenth century Australia had seethed with revolutionary fervour. And then the troops had been called out to put down the shearers' strike and the union leaders gaoled.

'They shall not say the fault is ours

If blood should stain the wattle.'

There was quite a militant strain in the Australian consciousness, in both the radicals and the reactionaries. It was only a century ago. And as Fullalove would say, if it worked once why wouldn't they do it again? Militias and arms dumps were not a totally inconceivable concept. Plant was almost beginning to believe in them.

And then he saw Madimi sitting at a café table talking to someone in khaki shorts and a purple t-shirt and a stylish Panama hat. At first he thought it might have been Uncle Toby, but when he looked again he saw that it was the clergyman from the memorial service. The purple t-shirt had a white rim round the neck which did duty for a dog collar. It looked like the regalia of a colonial bishop.

Maybe he had been promoted. Plant waited to cross the road to join them, but by the time a gap had opened in the traffic, the clergyman had finished his laying on of hands and Madimi had given him a farewell kiss, which he had reciprocated, and then Madimi was left sitting there alone as he disappeared round the corner into Jonson Street.

Ben Jonson had been a soldier, Plant recalled. He'd killed a man in a duel. His fellow playwright Marlowe had also killed someone in a fight; and had been an undercover agent, too. And then he had been killed in mysterious circumstances himself. There was no Marlowe Street. But there was a Marvell Street, and there were suspicions that he had been murdered by the Jesuits. There was also a Gordon Street, though there seemed no doubt that his suicide had been authentic. Rock Richmond's death, however it had occurred, was not something unique in the world of writing. Not if you took a historical perspective.

'Are you stalking me?' she asked.

'Not at all.'

'Not even personally, if not professionally?'

'Sorry,' Plant said, 'but no. Why would I do that?'

'Obsession,' she said. 'Or just keeping me under observation.'

'I observed you talking to the vicar,' Plant said.

'He's a sweetie.'

'Fresh fields to conquer?'

'He was offering me consolation.'

'Not hearing confession?'

'No. What have I got to confess?'

'You tell me.'

'Why would I tell you? You're not a priest. You can't

hear confession.'

'Nor can he. He's an Anglican.'

'So what?' she said.

'So you were confessing?'

'Not in the middle of the day in the middle of Byron,' she said.

'More a nocturnal kind of thing for the privacy of the home?' Plant suggested.

'I've no idea,' she said. 'My conscience is clear. How about yours?'

'Oh, absolutely,' Plant said.

'Did you ever find who took Rock's computer?' Madimi asked.

'No.'

'Did you find the back-ups?'

'No.'

'Did you look?'

'Not really.'

'Not really or not at all?'

'Rock didn't seem to be concerned. He just got me to contact the media in case the material showed up, and that was it.'

'That was it meaning that was all you did?'

'Yes.'

'Did he ever show you what he'd written? '

'No.'

'Did you ever read any of it?'

'No, how could I?'

'On the back-ups.'

'They'd been stolen.'

'What about the second set?'

What about them indeed? How did she know they existed?

'No idea. I never saw anything, anyway.'

'But he told you what he was writing.'

'Not really. He just said it was a sort of history of the alternative. But he didn't go into any detail.'

'Are you sure?'

'Sure I'm sure,' he said. 'I wasn't that interested, anyway.'

He could feel her gaze drilling into him. Over the years he had become used to that sensation. Act daft, his mother had always advised. And he hadn't been that interested in the little that Rock had told him. Fullalove's speculations had been far more interesting. And he wasn't going to be disclosing them to her, however enticing she made herself seem.

'Did you try and find out who it was?'

'Who did the break-in? No, he said not to bother. Just keep my ear to the ground in case I heard anything.'

'And did you?'

'Hear anything? No.'

'And did you keep your ear to the ground?'

'What is this? You checking to see if Rock overpaid me or something?'

'Show me your ear, Plant. Let me see if it's muddied.'

'It's not muddied. To be honest, I preferred to keep it clean. No one told me anything. No one seemed to care.'

'So you spoke to people.'

'Just the media people when I phoned around. But since I couldn't say whose material had gone missing, they weren't interested in knowing about it.'

'And you left it at that?'

'I didn't go round investigating, if that's what you mean.'

'You're sure?'

'Yes, I'm sure. Are you implying I should have done?'

'Not at all. What about Maggie?'

'She wasn't interested in Rock's writing to begin with. As I'm sure he told you. So she had no interest in finding out who took it. Or what he'd written,' he added for good measure.

'She hasn't asked you to ask around?'

'Not about the burglary.'

'About what then?'

'The circumstances of Rock's death.'

'And have you?'

'I could ask now, if you like.'

'Meaning what?'

'Are the police happy about your lack of alibi?'

'They simply loved it.'

'Isn't that nice?'

'I thought so.'

'How come they were so easily satisfied?'

'I didn't have to fuck them, if that's what you mean.'

'Was that a disappointment?'

'How could I say without knowing?'

'No past experience to go on?'

'What sort of girl do you think I am, Plant?'

'To be honest, I have no idea.'

'Honesty is the best policy, Plant.'

'Is that so?'

'Believe me,' she said.

'Now why on earth would I do that?' he asked.

'Do you want to come back to my place?' she asked.

'Then maybe I can show you.'

'Why not?' Plant asked.

There were several good reasons why not, but he chose to let them rest.

Chapter 32

Jake Illingworth was sitting in his Land Rover gazing out to sea as Plant came up from his morning walk on the beach. It seemed unlikely to be an accidental meeting. This was what came of being a creature of comparatively regular habits. People got to know your movements. People staked you out.

'I thought I recognised the vehicle,' Plant said.

'Classic British workmanship. None of that shoddy Japanese stuff. Who won the war, for heaven's sake?'

'Which war was that?' Plant asked. 'There are so many.'

'We need to talk,' Jake said.

'Sure. Whenever.'

'Fish place at Tweed Heads. We can do take-away and eat it in the park across the road.'

'Fine.'

'Unless you need a drink,' Jake added. 'Personally I don't drink in office hours.'

Maybe referring to office hours was his way of saying this was a business lunch. But a business lunch without drinking?

'I can live without it.'

'It's a lucky man who can say that,' Jake said. 'See you at twelve twenty.'

Plant seemed to recall reading that it was standard intelligence practice never to arrange to meet on the hour or half hour. And not to meet near your home base where people might know you or be watching out for you. Though it might simply be that it was Jake's favourite place for fish and chips. And that he shut the office precisely at noon and it was a twenty-minute drive. Precisely.

He gave Plant directions.

'Up the Pacific Highway and exit the freeway at Kennedy Drive. Take the underpass.'

Kennedy and the underpass. As in Dallas? Plant wondered. Was this going to be another day of reckoning?

Jake reversed down the track and turned.

When Plant arrived Jake was already there, sitting on a bench overlooking the water, eating his fish and chips and refusing to feed the seagulls. They stalked around and looked at him resentfully, even malevolently, but without effect. He was in the same vaguely military mufti, smart casual outfit; in addition he wore an American-style baseball hat, white with a long peak, the sort that protected you from having your face recorded on closed-circuit TV in gas stations and shopping malls. It had no distinguishing emblem or slogan. The Land Rover had slogans enough. Maybe he kept a second vehicle for secret trysts. A tourist boat advertising 'Catch a Crab' cruised quietly past the mangroves on the other side of the river. On the horizon Mount Warning signalled its usual admonition, its peak swallowed in cloud, like blindfolded justice.

'Here, have a chip,' Jake said.

Plant took one.

The seagulls squawked derisively.

'Thought it best to order,' Jake said. 'Less conspicuous than sitting around waiting. I recommend the local tailor. A lot of people dismiss it but personally I've always found it good value.'

Plant accepted the advice. It challenged his vegetarianism yet again, but in times of stress he allowed himself an intake of protein. He went in and placed his order and then joined Jake.

'Sorry if I seemed a bit curt on the beach,' Jake said. He took a swig from a bottle of still spring water. 'I didn't want anyone spotting us talking. That's why I suggested this place. You can sit here on the benches and see if anyone's approaching. Not the sort of place they'd have under regular surveillance. And if anyone shows up, you've already paid in advance so you can move on quickly. Not like being trapped inside a restaurant and having to wait for the bill.'

Plant nodded.

'I've been doing a bit of leg work. Thought I should bring you up to speed.'

'Thanks.'

'I've been checking out Maggie. She doesn't seem to have anyone on the side. You're the only chap I've seen call in there. I assume it was business.'

'Absolutely.'

No need to announce that he'd been fired and go into the circumstances of that.

'Can't say I like her or trust her but I can't see anything to suggest she killed Rock. I had a talk to her. I think she's clean. That Madimi creature's a different kettle of fish, though. Slippery as an eel.'

It seemed to be going to be another one of those fish theme conversations.

'Never took to her from the beginning. A chap's got to be realistic when you reach a certain age, you know.

I was in a shopping mall. This young girl was eyeing me off. Absolutely predatory. I thought I should be so lucky, and then I realised. It wasn't me she was fixing her beady gaze on, it was my sheepskin coat. Afghan. Absolutely authentic, picked it up in Kabul. She must have known. It was my pelt she wanted, not my body. You reach a certain age you've got to realise these things. Rock never did.'

He sighed for the vanished songs of yesteryear's spring.

'So this Madimi creature, she just suddenly appeared on the scene.'

'People do,' Plant said.

'Yes, I know. Got to start somewhere. But she appears out of nowhere and latches straight onto Rock. Like she came up here specially for him. Not like she arrived and scouted around for a bit. No, she's one determined piece of work. That's why I wanted us to meet covertly, you know. I don't want her staking us out.'

'But you're staking her out?'

'Doesn't mean she can't reciprocate.'

'And is she?'

'Is she what?'

'Reciprocating.'

'The reason I'm staking her out is because I make her for the sort of person who could be.'

'And what sort of person does that make her?'

Jake tugged at his moustache.

'A stalker, a psychopath, or someone like yourself?'

'Any of those,' Jake said, without asking Plant what Plant saw him as, or elucidating as to how he saw himself.

'So which is she? A crazed groupie or a professional killer? Or a professional groupie or an amateur killer?'

'That's what I hope to discover.'

'On your own or through your connections?'

'Yes,' Jake said.

'Yes?'

'Try both.'

'What if your connections are also her connections?'

He stroked his moustache some more.

'Could thicken the plot,' he said.

'Isn't it risky?'

'A chap's got to be able to handle risks. Risky in what way?'

'Well, presumably you're calling on your old SAS connections. What if she's one of their people? In these equal opportunity days?'

'Why should she be?'

'Rock's book.'

'What about Rock's book?'

'Did it touch on things?'

'What sort of things?'

'You tell me.'

He brooded. Did some more moustache tugging.

'It's an angle,' he said. 'I'd have to think about it.'

'You do that,' Plant recommended.

Chapter 33

Fullalove had been away for a couple of days. Plant had returned from his amorous adventures to find the house empty, and it never filled up again. He sat on his verandah wondering idly about where Fullalove might be. It was quite pleasant sitting there alone. It was why he had left the city in the first place, to be away from things. More specifically, to be away from people. The firetails and the finches and the crested wrens darted in and out of the bushes. The pigeons trampled around in the tops of the camphor laurels. He could not decide whether Fullalove had simply wandered off or should be posted missing. And if missing, what should he do about it? With Fullalove you never knew. He might have found himself a playmate. He couldn't recollect Fullalove ever having had one, but who could tell? Beneath that rough exterior who knew what rough beast lurked. He might not appreciate being found. Nor was Plant unhappy to have him lost. Fullalove's disappearance was both convenient and inconvenient. Indeed he was delighted Fullalove had left. He welcomed the return of his home, his privacy, his life. But at the same time there was the inconvenience of the worry. He could not simply enjoy Fullalove's absence: he worried about looking for him, whether he should. And the where, how, and how dangerous. If Fullalove had been abducted rather than just wandered off, this might be dangerous stuff. In the end he just did nothing, on the principle that something would turn up. It did.

'We have a Mr Fullalove here,' said the voice on the end of the line. 'He said you would vouch for him and pick him up.'

'Pick him up where?'

'At the station, sir,' said the voice, identifying itself as from the local police.

'What's he done? Do I have to raise bail?'

'No, that won't be necessary.'

'Is he under arrest?'

'No, I don't think it's come to that, sir. If you come down here I'm sure somebody will explain. We did offer to run him back but he said you'd prefer it this way.'

'Yes,' Plant said. He certainly preferred it this way. Anything rather than having your friendly neighbourhood cop dropping in.

'I'll be right down,' he said.

Nevertheless, before he left he emptied out the ash from the shells into the slow combustion stove and then rinsed them in the sink, hid his stash in one of the herbal tea jars in the kitchen, cleared away the cigarette papers and tucked them in the drawer beneath his socks, checked Fullalove's room and put his papers and dope beneath the mattress and opened all the windows to air the house. It probably wouldn't help if they came through with sniffer dogs but it made him feel he'd at least tried to do something.

'So what happened, where've you been?' Plant asked.

'Tell you later,' Fullalove said.

They got in the car.

'So tell me,' Plant said.

'Tell you later,' Fullalove said. 'I need a shower and a change of clothes.'

It had to be serious. Fullalove had never been one to be overly concerned about such things as showers and clean clothes.

'So did you ...?'

'Tell you later,' Fullalove said. He put the radio on full blast. 'Don't want to talk about it now.' He raised a finger in front of his lips.

'Fair enough,' Plant said.

'So,' Plant said, as Fullalove sat wrapped in towels, rolling a smoke on the verandah.

'Later,' Fullalove said.

He got himself dressed finally and came outside again.

'Let's go for a walk,' Fullalove said.

It was most uncharacteristic.

'Let's go.'

Plant locked up. Fullalove headed for the car.

'I thought you wanted to walk.'

'The beach,' Fullalove said, pretty well *sotto voce*.

'Whatever you say,' Plant said.

'And then pick up my ute.'

'Let's go down by the waves,' Fullalove said.

'Sure. You need to inhale some ozone?'

'Just the noise of them,' Fullalove said. 'Should make it harder to pick anything up.'

'Pick what up?'

'Sound,' Fullalove said, when they reached the edge of the surf. 'Bugs.'

'I take it you're not referring to sand-flies and midges.'

'Too right I'm not.'

'I don't think anyone would be bugging the beach.'

'You don't know what happened,' Fullalove said. 'I reckon it's safer than the house. Or the car.'

'So what happened?'

'She killed him,' Fullalove said.

'Who?'

'Your little friend. She shot Illingworth.'

'Jake? Is he dead?'

'Sure is.'

'Who says?'

'I do.'

'How do you know?'

'I was there, man.'

Plant stopped. 'Are you serious?'

'Just keep walking,' Fullalove said, looking round, checking out the empty beach, the deserted dunes, the untravelled sea.

'So what happened?'

'She came into Illingworth's office and blew his brains out.'

'Were you there?'

'I was locked up in this cell he's got there in back of the office.'

'A cell?'

'Looks like a storeroom but in effect it's a neat little cell. No window. No outside access. Solid door in a metal frame. And I don't think it was designed as a storeroom, either. Not with the steel loops cemented into the wall.'

'Probably just to hang stuff from.'

'Yeah. Like prisoners. Victims.'

'With markings on the wall? The days marked off by previous occupants?'

'Couldn't see. There wasn't any light. Or if there was

he never switched it on. Beneath that smiling, ginger face lurked a full-on psychopath.'

'So how do you know she killed him?'

'I heard her, man.'

'And she didn't hear you in your cell?'

'She never checked it out. You wouldn't know it was there, you'd think it was just a storeroom. She just fired a couple of shots and then sat down at the computer.'

'You could see her?'

'No, I was in this pitch-black cell, but I could hear her. Hear that electronic noise the computer makes to let you know it's booting up.'

'How do you know it was her?'

'He spoke to her, didn't he? He says, "Hullo, Madimi, what can I do for you?" and she says "Hello, Jake" and then phut. And a few minutes later another shot.'

'Two shots.'

'Yeah, I figure she killed him with the first shot and then she put the gun in his hand and fired a second shot into a block of wood or something to get his prints on the gun and some gunshot residue on his hand. Then she sits down at the computer and writes a suicide note. Presumably she took the block away with her and tossed it in the bush somewhere. In the Brunswick river or something. I think you'll find that it will turn out to be the same gun that killed Rock Richmond. No way to prove it wasn't Jake's. The police will assume it's just some unregistered gun he happened to have, along with all his registered ones, souvenired from active service or enemy hands like soldiers always do. '

'How do you know if you couldn't see anything?'

'I could hear the printer printing it out.'

'She printed out a suicide note?'

'So the cops were saying. Except they thought Jake wrote it.'

'They told you?'

'No, I heard them talking.'

'Did they believe your story?'

'What story?'

'That she wrote it.'

'No way, man, I didn't tell them anything. You think I want to get myself killed? You think I want to have her visiting one night? As far as the cops are concerned I was locked up in the storeroom and I didn't hear or see anything. No one came, no one went. I told them I'd been drugged. I said he fed me funny cookies and I passed out and then next thing I know there's cops all over the office and I call out to them. Made noises anyway, couldn't talk since he'd gagged me.'

'Who called the cops?'

'Some fishermen. Couldn't get any reply from the office, looked through the window, saw Jake slumped there and phoned the police.'

'And they found you in the storeroom.'

'In the cell, yes. Bound, gagged and drugged.'

'Did they believe you?'

'There was enough residual THC in my system to show up on the saliva test, I reckon.'

'And they didn't think you'd killed him.'

'Well, since I was bound and gagged and locked up with the bolts on the outside it's a bit hard to figure how I could have. Even for cops. No, they think he killed himself. I told them the guy was a maniac and they seemed to buy that. They reckon I was lucky to be alive. So do I. They think he killed your Rock Richmond and then offed himself.'

'Why do they think that?'

'That's what the note said. Killed Rock Richmond and then killed himself from remorse.'

'Why would he have done that?'

'Well, he didn't, did he?'

'But he must have given a reason.'

'Not if he didn't write it.'

'But she must have given a reason to make it sound convincing.'

'Well I didn't see it, did I? I just heard the cops talking. They weren't exactly going to hand it across to me and say "Is this what you heard her printing out?"'

'And they didn't say what reason he gave.'

'No, they didn't say. I imagine she wrote something like it was a personal matter. She wasn't going to be drawing attention to the book of revelations they were writing.'

'I guess not.'

'There you are then. Just keep it simple. Easier for everyone all round. Who cares about his motive? Especially when there was no motive since he didn't do it. No point in making it too complicated and arousing doubts and suspicions. He just did it. He was a nutter. He'd been on active service. Gets to them all in the end. Post-traumatic stress disorder. '

'So how did you explain how you were there? Didn't they think it was odd?'

'I said I was a journalist writing a piece about the late great Rock Richmond. I'd called in to interview Illingworth and he must have got paranoid and thought I'd found out he'd killed Rock or something. So he slipped me a couple of cookies and tied me up.'

'Why did he kill Rock?'

'Well he didn't, did he? Don't be ridiculous. Your little playmate did.'

'How do you know that?'

'Because he told me.'

'Who told you?'

'Jake Illingworth, who do you think? Think I was communing with the dead? Summoning up the ghost of Rock Richmond? Spare me. You can keep your little spirit friends.'

'So when did he tell you? How did he know?'

'He found me. He was good, I'll give him that. Very quick, very quiet. I was staking out the caravan park and suddenly he jumps me. Didn't hear a thing. I don't know how he knew I was there. But he did. He'd been waiting. He thought I'd come after him.'

'Well, you had.'

'No, mate. He thought I'd come to kill him. After Rock was killed he figured he was next on the list. It was lucky he decided to grill me first. Could've just killed me. He was strong, too. Got me into his office and put the cuffs on me. He had all the gear. Then he started the grilling. Like I'd been put in Guantánamo Bay. Wanted to know who I was, what I was doing.'

'And you told him?'

'You bet I told him. He was seriously professional. He'd done this stuff before, no point fucking around. So I said I was helping you out.'

'Thanks, mate.'

'No need to worry, he's dead now. He won't be coming after you. I told him Rock had hired you to find his missing files and then Mrs Rock hired you to find out who killed him. And I said you reckoned there was a militia angle that someone didn't want being made public and someone stole the files.'

'You said that? That was your theory, not mine.'

'Same difference. Look, this guy was seriously psychopathic. He had me manacled in this cell. No windows. No light. There was only one thing to do, that was level with him.'

'So you levelled with him and he locked you up.'

'He was starting to believe me. I said you figured it was Mrs Rock or him killed Rock.'

'You said that?'

'Don't keep interrupting,' Fullalove complained. 'You want me to tell you, then let me tell you. I said you figured out given motive and opportunity and means it was him or her. He said it wasn't him and he'd checked out her and didn't reckon she'd done it. He figured it was Rock's little playmate. I didn't tell him she was your little playmate, too.'

'Why did he think it was Madimi?'

'The way he figured it, they'd hired her to plug the leaks. Someone had heard Rock was writing this book. Which wasn't hard since he seemed to have told everyone he ever met he was writing it. And someone didn't want certain things getting out. They put her onto him and she played the wide-eyed groupie let me sit at your feet, oh great writer, and come into bed with me.'

'Did he know this for sure?'

'He was working on it. He thought I might have been on her team. I tried to tell him I wasn't. Not my type. He said he'd have to hold onto me till he'd got a few things worked out. But she beat him to it. He was professional, mate, but she's something else again. Your little friend is a killer, Plant. Talk about unsafe sex.'

Plant could feel the chill. There was no point arguing about it. At the deepest level he suspected Fullalove was right.

'So why did she kill Illingworth?'

'Because he'd been working with Rock on the book. He knew all the stuff on the secret militias. So she had to eliminate him too so nothing ever came out. Lucky she didn't think you knew what they'd been up to. Saved your life.'

It was more than a chill that Plant felt. A veritable ice-age enveloping him.

'You all right?' Fullalove asked.

'Just a goose walking over my grave.'

'Well at least you're not in it yet.'

That was true. He preferred not to dwell on how close it had been.

'How did Illingworth know she'd killed Rock?'

'He didn't for sure. But he'd spotted your little so-called spirit friend was some sort of young spook when she was first onto Rock. And then she came and visited him.'

'I knew it wasn't for my body,' Jake had told Fullalove. 'When you've done as many interrogations as I've done, you know when someone's doing it to you. What she wanted to know, pretty clearly, was whether I was working with Rock on writing his book, or whether Rock was running with it on his own. I don't think he would have told her any of the sensitive stuff, but I couldn't be sure. Pillow talk. No fool like an old fool. I could see that glint in her eye. Like she'd like to wire me up to a polygraph machine. Stick electrodes on my testicles. No way I was letting her into my bed, make my morning coffee and slip me some sodium pentothal. Like I said, I knew all those old tricks. Been there, done that. Of course there might've been some new ones I didn't know. So I was very wary of her.'

'But he just wasn't wary enough,' Fullalove said.

'And he told you about the militias?' Plant said. 'And the arms caches?'

'Not in so many words.'

'What does that mean?'

'A matter of deduction. He was officer class. They don't give out secrets. Just name, rank and serial number. He wasn't saying anything. I guess he wanted to keep it for the book. Now Rock was dead he was going to write it himself. If you'd played your cards right you could have got yourself a ghost-writing job.'

'Or got myself killed.'

'Like I said, ghost-writing.'

'How do you know he wanted to do the book?'

'He told me.'

'Really?'

'As good as. That's why he hassled Mrs Rock about whether Rock had kept a second back-up somewhere.'

'So you still don't know for sure there ever were any militias. There still isn't any evidence.'

'There wouldn't be any evidence.'

'So how do you know?'

'It's obvious. Logic. Human nature. Comparative history.'

'And now Jake's dead.'

'Someone still has to be running it.'

'But no one knows. Not even you.'

'The people in it know.'

'But no one else.'

'What's the point of a secret operation if people know about it? That's why they sent your little friend round killing people. To keep it secret.'

A helicopter came low over the beach out of nowhere, following the line of the surf. Fullalove rolled his eyes upward in silent gesture and stopped talking. It was insane. Plant remembered a helicopter there from once before, when? It was that morning he had first spotted Madimi on the beach. The morning she had spotted him, maybe. It was insane but it was all insane. He felt the chill return. Anything was possible.

The helicopter passed out of earshot and finally out of sight.

Fullalove offered his scenario. How far it was based on what Jake had told Fullalove, and how far it was Fullalove's interpretation, there was no way for Plant to know.

Chapter 34

Jake Illingworth had begun to doubt. It didn't need to be spelled out any more than that. Gradually, irrevocably, he had come not to believe. Not to believe in the wisdom of his masters: not the army, no, he still believed in that, the instrument, the surgical implement. But he no longer trusted his political masters. He no longer believed they had the welfare of the nation at heart. All they cared for was what they could get out of it. They were for sale to the highest bidder. At the moment the highest bidder was the USA, and he had no belief in the wisdom of the political masters of that country, either. Vietnam in retrospect seemed more than ever to have been a mistake. And nothing had been learned. Afghanistan, Iraq, Libya, Syria: it was all misguided, mismanaged, ill-informed. And for what? It was a record of destruction and greed. The system no longer had his loyalty. That was frightening for an army officer. It took him into regions that he feared. To avoid looking ahead he looked back. And wondered what it had all been about. He talked about it with Rock, who felt equally at odds with the present political world. They began looking over the past they had known. They recuperated what they had shared. The idea of writing it all down, to see where it had gone wrong, was something they came up with together. It had begun as a way of reaching understanding. It developed into a crusade and a vision of wealth and glory. Their due rewards might still be theirs. What held them back from claiming them?

He was not specific about it; it was all rather rhetorical, the specific was embedded there and awaiting decoding. He was still cautious about what he said. But he was beginning to erect the signposts. He was still bound by the Secrets Act he had signed, but he could hint, suggest, offer veiled analysis, historic parallels.

He felt not exactly betrayed. But let down at least. Abandoned. Like Rock. Here they were, good establishment old boys, from good old establishment backgrounds. They had put in their time. And what was there to show for it? The army pension hardly offered largesse. The Australia First Caravan Park was not markedly thriving. Maybe he had expected to pick up some odd jobs. A spell of interrogation in Iraq. But it didn't happen. Like Rock, he was no longer needed. And in turn he didn't feel that much loyalty to his masters.

And then living up amongst the alternative all those years, the alternative values had got to him. It was always the case. Drug squad detectives would go undercover, drop a few tabs of acid, ingest a few magic mushrooms and start thinking, hey, this is the life, who wants to be straight? KGB operatives got into bed with the West and bought the allures of capitalism and sold out the Soviet Union.

So he started thinking, these militias, whose side were they going to be on, when the time came to use them? Whose side was he going to be on, for that matter? He began to doubt the strategy of putting down insurgents. He began to feel it was the politicians needed putting down. He no longer believed in the terrorist threat. Real terrorists would be putting down politicians, not random, innocent civilians. He began to think the terrorists were being used; he began to think that he was being used; used by his political masters. He and Rock would sit around yarning, share a few joints, and think, there has to be something better. Let's make some serious money out of all the stuff they knew. It was not a mission from God. Whether or not they believed in God, they no longer believed in the code of the officer class, loyalty to the government, preserving the secrecy they had agreed to. They were totally disillusioned with government, so disillusioned they were not even concerned to make a political exposé, and without any compunctions about revealing whatever they knew. The motivation was money, fame, celebrity. Just a story to sell. The truth about the alternative, the secret history of the communes.

'After Rock got burgled, they still carried on working. They got all gung-ho. We shall not surrender.'

'And Madimi found out.'

'Rock told her. He was besotted. Couldn't wait to tell her everything. Seems she had that effect on men.'

'How do you know that?'

'Don't bother disputing it,' Fullalove said.

'I asked how you know.'

'Observation,' Fullalove said.

'Observation.'

'And information received.'

Plant waited for him to say first-hand experience. But Fullalove was never one to reveal his sources.

'So how did Madimi get into the act?' Plant asked.

'Security must have heard what Rock was up to and put her on the case.'

'Would they have heard?'

'If I heard, then they would have.'

'You heard?'

'Of course. What do you think I came up here for?'

'How did you hear?'

'You hear things,' Fullalove said. 'Rock obviously couldn't stop himself from telling people what he was working on. And instead of taking the hint and shutting up when he got burgled he got even more excited. Must have made him feel important. Somebody wanting his deathless prose.'

'So what did you come up here for?'

'Smelled a story, didn't I? Make my name.'

'I thought you came up to hide out for a while. Get away from certain people.'

'Yeah, well.'

'Now you're saying you came up for a story.'

'No law against doing a couple of things at the same time.'

Plant wondered, not for the first time, just how far Fullalove was a lone operator. Freelance, or hired help? Could he be working for the secret state? Somebody else's secret state? If the survivalist militias were really out there, who had been funding them? Australia or the Americans? Maybe Fullalove had a watching brief, but on whose behalf? Or was that just being paranoid and uncharitable? How could you tell in this post post-modern world? How could you ever know the simple truth in a climate of institutionally mandatory pluralism?

'So will it make your name? This story?'

Fullalove laughed, bitterly.

'No way, mate. No way this story gets written up. No one knows Illingworth told me anything,' Fullalove said. 'In fact he didn't tell me anything. He hinted, but he never actually said it. No one even needs to know I was there when he got killed. The police will treat it as a suicide.'

'You reckon?'

'Not a doubt,' Fullalove said.

'And you didn't tell them it was Madimi?'

'Are you crazy? No way I'm saying anything.'

'So it'll be seen as suicide.'

'Sure. Special Branch or the Feds or ASIO or someone will have a word to them just to make sure. Maybe some organisation we've never even heard of. Your little friend will be spirited away. Nothing will ever come out. Let's just keep it like that. Suits me.'

'If you say so,' Plant said.

'If anyone knows you know this, we'll both be dead.'

'Thank you for nothing,' Plant said.

'Yes, well, mate, I don't care about you especially, but I certainly want to live.'

'Thanks again,' Plant said. 'Is this an official warning?'

'Official warning?'

'That's what it sounds like.'

'Well, mate, why not take it like that? Just to be on the safe side.'

'Yes,' Plant said. 'I think I will.'

'Good man,' Fullalove said.

'So where's Madimi now?' Plant asked.

'Guantánamo Bay, no doubt. Or Baghdad. Kabul maybe. Off sinking Greenpeace boats in New Zealand or shooting IRA types in Gibraltar or blowing up Palestinians. There's no shortage of work for a girl like her. Seconded to our allies. Or maybe they seconded her to us. It's hard to tell where they originally come from with those private school accents.'

Chapter 35

Plant bought takeaway Indonesian. Gado-gado, Balinese fried noodles, red basil curry with tofu.

'So much for survivalism,' Fullalove said.

'Take-away is survivalism in its own way,' Plant said. 'It's learning how to survive in existing conditions. This is the condition of society.'

'Indonesian takeaway.'

'Exactly. And you adjust to it. Why make it hard for yourself?'

They hoed into the noodles. At least Fullalove had no objection to eating vegetarian; he would eat anything. But he had objections to everything else. He was in an irritated, restive, picky frame of mind. Incarceration seemed not to have agreed with him.

'This shell collecting thing, man, I reckon its some kind of sick fetish. Don't you think you should get it treated? It can't be healthy. Just the smell of them. You ought to boil them, or something. Get the rotting marine matter off them.'

Plant looked at his beautiful collection along the windowsills. Boil them. He shuddered at the thought of it.

'You don't think you ought to get some, like, medical advice? All these shell shapes. Very suggestive. Mounds of Venus. These cowries. Very feminine. And then there's the corkscrew ones. And the intimate colours. Delicate sort of come into my bower you little bit of grit and I will turn you into a pearl. You don't think you ought to get like some Freudian help, maybe?'

'No,' Plant said.

'No?'

'No.'

'Suit yourself. You're sure you don't have a problem with female sexuality?'

'Get fucked,' Plant said.

'I rest my case,' Fullalove said.

But Plant knew Fullalove never rested any case. Bit by bit he was casting his baleful urban glance on everything and destroying it.

'Tell me,' he tried again, 'have you ever actually solved a crime?'

'Of course,' Plant said.

'Brought the villain to justice?' Fullalove said.

'I'm not a bounty hunter.'

'Never thought you were. You don't have the build for it.'

'I do investigations,' Plant said. Irritably. Fullalove could be immensely irritating, sitting sneering there over his red curry.

'Research assistance, investigative reporting,' Fullalove said.

'Yes.'

'It's on your card.'

'I know. I put it there.'

'But what does it actually mean?'

'It means I research and investigate and report back.'

'Report back what?'

'What I've discovered.'

'And what do you discover?'

'What do you mean, what do I discover?'

'Do you ever find out who done it?'

'Yes.'

'Always?'

'Look,' Plant said, 'I report back to my clients what I find. It's up to them to assess how they want to interpret it.'

'So it needs interpreting?'

'Sometimes.'

'Often?'

'Quite often. Things aren't always clear-cut. Sometimes the client hasn't filled me in on the whole picture.'

'So it's a matter of interpreting what you've dug up.'

'Of course.'

'Which isn't, as you say, always clear-cut.'

'Not always.'

'You've learned to live with doubt?'

'Look,' Plant said, 'I'm hired to find out what I can find out. I'm not an arresting officer. I'm not a prosecutor. I just hand over what I know.'

'So sometimes things might not get resolved.'

'Sometimes.'

'Sometimes there's an area of ambiguity.'

'There's always ambiguity.'

'So you could say that sometimes in the end you don't actually know.'

'You could.'

'And do you?'

'Do I what? Know it or say it?'

'Whichever,' Fullalove said. 'So this case, mate, isn't really an exception. It's just par for the course.'

'What are you getting at?'

'The fact that in the end you never did find out what it

was all about. It's not sort of untypical for you. So no one's going to be saying anything. Least of all you. Are you?'

'No,' Plant said.

'Good,' Fullalove said. 'I'd just make sure to keep it that way, if I were you. The stuff about Illingworth, you won't be reporting that back to the widow.'

'Is that another order?'

'Just a health warning.'

'Who are you working for, Fullalove?' Plant asked, not especially hopeful of getting an answer. Fullalove might not even know, anyway. Could have been hired with a number of cut-outs in place.

'Who would employ me?' Fullalove replied.

And that was it.

The frogs croaked down by the creek. A couple of owls hooted along the valley.

'It's so noisy,' Fullalove complained. 'Listen to it. All the time. Birds hooting. Dogs barking. Things on the roof. All day long there's chain saws. Brush cutters. Tractors. Trail bikes. Bobcats. Whip birds. Mowers. Bulldozers. Cows.'

'Just the sounds of nature,' Plant said.

'I don't know how you stand it.'

Sometimes Plant felt as if Fullalove deliberately set out to destabilise him. But it was just the dark before the dawn, and the dawn came.

'I've had it, mate, that's it.'

'That's it?'

'I'm heading back to the city. Get some peace and quiet.'

Plant's heart leapt up.

'I'd rather deal with the villains there than the types you've got in the wilds out here.'

'It's not exactly wild.'

'It is as far as I'm concerned.'

Plant did not try to discourage him.

Plant sat on the beach and watched the crabs emerge cautiously from their holes, wait motionless with their eyes just protruding over the top, and then scuttle out to deposit a load of sand from their subterranean excavations and as rapidly disappear. The beach was crisscrossed with the tracks of their claws, intersecting sometimes with the footprints of seagulls. He sat gazing at the tracks as if they were lines of hieroglyphs that might be read. As the day went on dogs and horses and humankind would add to them.

He wondered what, if any of it, was true. As Fullalove had predicted, the police and the coroner and whoever else was in on it had agreed that Jake Illingworth had committed suicide while the balance of his mind was disturbed, having previously murdered Rock Richmond, as his suicide note had stated. It was a neat solution to a couple of killings, but was there any reason to believe it? But was there any reason to believe Fullalove's version? There was only Fullalove's word to go on that Madimi had killed Jake, and as far as Plant knew he was the only person to whom that word had been delivered. Could Fullalove have made that up? Well, yes, easily. But why? There seemed no obvious reason. Was he trying to discourage Plant from dallying with her? Fullalove had never been one to offer warning on dalliances before. Was Fullalove somehow involved in it all? It was not impossible. But in that case why would he have fingered Madimi?

Plant cruised past her house. There was a For Lease sign outside. He called in at the real estate agent. She had never heard of a Madimi Dee. A Mr Walsingham had rented the house for his daughter Matilda but she had since moved away.

Plant asked how long ago was since.

'I can't tell you,' she said. 'But the house has only just come back on our books.'

He asked how recently was only just?

'This weekend.'

He asked if the daughter was still around.

She didn't know. Nor could she say if the daughter was in Australia. Mr Walsingham lived in the Cayman Islands. Or at least he banked there. Would Plant like to look the property over?

'A bit outside my price range,' he said.

'I'll ask if we can come down a bit.'

Plant shook his head and tried wriggling out of that one. The agent asked for his mobile number. He told her he didn't have a mobile.

'Land-line, then,' she said.

'Let me think about it and I'll call you back,' he offered, but she was adamant.

He made up a number at random with the local prefix and she wrote it down.

'And your name?' she asked before he could get out of the door.

'Oates,' he said. 'Toby Oates.'

Chapter 36

Maggie phoned.

'You heard the news? Everything solved. Jake the murderer. I must say I never did take to him. So since that's all tidied up and I no longer need to hire you, why don't you come round here now I'm not a client anymore? I hear your little spirit friend has evaporated into the ether so I imagine you've lots of time on your hands. And your other appendages. So get round here, Plant. Now.'

He did as he was told.

'So you've your mislaid your little friend, Plant.'

'Which little friend is that?'

'How many have you got?'

'You tell me who you had in mind.'

'Miss Layladylay. The doleful Dolores, Our Lady of Pain. I hear she's not around any more.'

'How did you hear that?'

'Never you mind.'

'Yes, well, she seems to have disappeared.'

'Meaning what?'

'Vanished.'

'Interesting. Ran off, did she?'

'She doesn't seem to be around, anyway.'

'You checked?'

Plant shrugged.

'I know you did, Plant. You went down to the real estate agent and asked for a forwarding address. No need to look startled. There's not much goes on in this shire I don't find out about, Plant. Worth your while to remember that.'

'I certainly will,' he said.

'So why were you doing that?'

'Just following up my inquiries.'

'And how far did your inquiries get?'

'They've come to an end.'

'Is that so?' she said. 'Personally, I wouldn't be surprised if she didn't kill the two of them.'

'Which two?'

'Jake and Rock, of course. Are there any more?'

'Not that I know of.'

'So did she?'

'It's not impossible.'

'No, it's not, is it?'

'The police don't think so, however.'

'Well, they wouldn't, would they?'

He didn't ask what she meant.

'What other little friend did you think I meant you'd mislaid?' she asked.

'Fullalove's gone, too.'

'I hope you're not inconsolable.'

'Not at all.'

'It's not like losing a husband, after all.'

'No.'

'Or is it?'

'No.'

'Well, that's a relief.'

'Nothing like that,' Plant assured her.

'So you could be consolable. Open to some tender loving female care?'

'Where would I get it?' Plant asked.

'I can never work out whether you're deliberately

offensive or just crass,' she said.

'That's what Fullalove used to say.'

She gave him a hard and steely look. Yes, there was no doubt, she could have been quite capable of killing Rock. And Jake. Poor Rock, caught between Maggie and Madimi. Poor Plant for that matter. Unemployed too, facing impoverishment again.

'If you play your cards right I might be able to persuade the firm to put some work your way. I imagine you need it. Check out the background for some of our cases. How does that strike you?'

It struck him once again that she seemed to have developed psychic powers. Or she'd been checking up on his tax returns and bank statements. Or both.

'Plant!' she snapped at him. 'Answer me.'

Books by Michael Wilding from Arcadia and Australian Scholarly

THE PRISONER OF MOUNT WARNING

ISBN 978192 1509568

'With a detective called Plant and a journey from Sydney to the dope fields of Byron Bay, the private eye novel has come a long way from Raymond Chandler ... the detective novel's move into an era of magic mushrooms and free love.' – *Sydney Morning Herald*.

'This satirical odyssey from an Australian literary legend has his protagonist heading north to find himself, among other things. Charles Dorritt recovers from a breakdown by doing a writing course and decides to write of his torture and slavery at the hands of the security services. He's pursued by Plant, who's been hired to dissuade him from revealing all... Wilding was at the forefront of a rebellious Australian literary movement in the '70s; in this book, he weaves a narrative of personal, literary and political dimensions into an entertaining yarn.' – Phil Brown, *Brisbane News*.

THE MAGIC OF IT

ISBN 978192 1875373

'The truth in this fiction is at least as entertaining as what has been invented. This a clever, offbeat rendering of a crime story with a smattering of illustrations by the great Australian artist Garry Shead and a protagonist who surely will be back.' – Emma Young, *Sydney Morning Herald*.

'With his previous Plant novel, *The Prisoner of Mount Warning*, Michael Wilding broke new ground. Plant investigates, not the petty individual crimes like kidnapping, murder or extortion, but the big picture – the intellectual and political follies of the age. True to the genre, Plant's cases start small and grow but, unlike the books in which the bodies pile up, with Wilding the unstable underpinning of modern industrialised society is laid bare. And made hilariously funny.' – Peter Corris.

ASIAN DAWN
ISBN 978192 1875397

'A compelling narrative with a cast of enigmatic figures. The exotic bar singer, the speech writer for hire, the publisher with guerrilla connections, the sex-addicted expatriate and the missing political scientist are only some of the fascinating cast of characters ... Wilding blends his wit with the comic and the bizarre in a novel that surprises by its twists and turns. This is a novel that enhances our understanding of the Australian-Asian relationship while at the same time providing an exciting, fast-moving thriller.' – Irina Dunn, *Network News.*

'*Asian Dawn* is a fast-paced read with lots of seedy sex and compromising secrets, plus a few well aimed jabs at the academic world.' – Cameron Woodhead, *Sydney Morning Herald.*

IN THE VALLEY OF THE WEED
ISBN 978192 5333978

'The Plant novels, of which this is the fifth ... are hybrids of satire and crime fiction, too funny to be called bleak, but concealing a complex seriousness of purpose. At the instigation of his old friend Fullalove, Plant in his capacity as private detective goes looking for an academic who has been suspended for thoughtcrime and has subsequently disappeared. The least attractive aspects of neoliberalism and its consequences come in for some savage critique in this intermittently hilarious novel.' – Kerryn Goldsworthy, *The Age.*

WILD BLEAK BOHEMIA:
MARCUS CLARKE, ADAM LINDSAY GORDON
AND HENRY KENDALL:
A DOCUMENTARY

ISBN 978192 5003802

Winner of the Prime Minister's Literary Award for non-fiction and the Colin Roderick Award.

'A superb study of colonial culture ... Wilding's splendid book,' – Peter Pierce, *Weekend Australian.*

'This wonderful book ... this outstanding, original documentary,' – Patrick Morgan, *Quadrant.*

'A remarkable exercise in literary history ... an extraordinarily rich picture,' – Paul de Serville, *Newtown Review of Books.*

GROWING WILD

ISBN 978192 5333107

'This entertaining, instructive memoir by veteran Australian writer and publisher Michael Wilding ... a memoir of one particular life and also of the milieus and movements it intersected with and animated: those of scholars, academics, poets, fiction writers, anarchists and activists, in various permutations. *Growing Wild* is the memory of someone who always took notice, and always took notes.' – Inez Baranay, *Newtown Review of Books.*

'An important historical record of a seminal period in Australian writing, as well as a revealing insight into the life and mind of a writer ... It is both an entertaining and visionary book on how to sustain a literary life and at the same time remain true to key intellectual values and beliefs.' – Ross Fitzgerald, *Weekend Australian.*